Girl's Luck Runs Out

An Ella Porter Mystery Thriller

Georgia Wagner

Contents

Prologue

The rotting wooden beams of the abandoned tavern creaked under their own weight as if the building was taking its final dying breaths. Dusty cobwebs dangled from every corner, clinging to the peeling, yellow wallpaper that was curling at the edges.

A building that ought to have been abandoned was now occupied by two souls.

A young woman, no more than twenty, tried to escape the grip of the man.

Panic flooded her senses as she struggled against him, screaming until her throat burned. It was no use. She was trapped.

She screamed again, thrashing with all her might, but his grip only tightened. He dragged her across the room and through a doorway into utter blackness. The wooden floorboards gave way to dirt. They were descending into some kind of cellar.

Panic clawed at her insides. She couldn't see anything, couldn't get her bearings. The musty air was dank and stifling.

"Please," she sobbed. "Please let me go."

His breath hissed against her ear. "Not a chance."

The cellar door banged shut above them, shrouding them in pitch darkness. She stumbled on the uneven steps, clinging to his arm to keep from tumbling headfirst.

At the bottom, he released his hold on her wrist only to shove her against a wall. Frigid, jagged stones bit into her back. She shrieked in terror.

"Feisty little thing, aren't you?" His voice held a mocking lilt. "I do enjoy a challenge."

She drove her knee upward, rewarded by a satisfying grunt of pain. But her triumph was short-lived. A hard blow struck her cheek, snapping her head to the side. Warm blood trickled from her mouth.

Through the haze of pain and fear, she heard the scrape of a match and saw a flicker of light in the darkness.

In the pale glow of the match, she glimpsed her captor's face for the first time. Her eyes widened in horror.

"Not nice to stare," he whispered.

She stumbled away from him, shoving off his chest.

Her heart pounded as she strained to see in the pitch blackness. She had to get out of here. Now.

She groped blindly along the wall, scraping her hands on the rough stones, searching for a door or window. Anything. There—a sliver of light peeked from under a door. She lunged for the handle and yanked with all her might. Locked.

Panic rose in her chest. She pounded on the thick wood and screamed for help until her throat was raw, but no one came. Exhaustion and despair threatened to overwhelm her.

Then she heard a faint creak behind her. She whirled around just as a match flared again, illuminating a hideous grin. "No one can hear you down here, girlie."

She glimpsed a hat pulled low over dark eyes and a coat buttoned up to the chin—but little else to identify her captor. He took a step toward her, match flickering, features twisted into a malevolent sneer.

In his other hand, he held something odd.

A dart.

She stared at it, breathing heavily.

He was extending the item towards her.

"Wanna play?"

She swallowed.

"W-what..." Her mind was racing, trying to make sense of any of it. But none of it computed.

He pointed with the dart at a board on the wall. "We play. You score a bullseye, you live. You miss, you die. Deal?"

Horror welled in her chest.

Adrenaline shot through her veins. She snatched the dart from his hand and hurled it at his face.

The match went out. A roar of rage echoed through the darkness, followed by the sound of heavy boots striking the floorboards. She scrambled away, heart pounding, as he charged blindly after her. His fingers grazed her arm, then caught on her sleeve.

She twisted and squirmed with all her might, tearing the fabric to escape his grasp. His curses rang out behind her as she groped her way to the far wall. If she could just find another door or a window—

A loud bang shook the cellar. She shrieked as the overhead light flickered on, revealing her captor standing by the switch, dart in hand. His hat was askew and his cheek bore an angry red mark—but his eyes glinted with triumph. "You can't escape me, girlie. Now, shall we continue our little game?"

She shook her head frantically, backing into a corner. "Please, just let me go. I won't tell anyone, I swear—"

"I'm afraid it's too late for that." He strode toward her, rolling the dart between his fingers.

Panic rose in her chest as he approached. She glanced around for a weapon, anything she could use to defend herself, but the cellar was bare.

He grabbed her arm, yanking her toward the dart board again. "Three shots," he said. "Actually," he spat, rubbing at his cheek, "Let's make it two. You wasted one."

She tried to shout, but he just shook his head like a disappointed father.

"Scream all you like. No one will hear you."

She stood trembling in front of the dart board, wishing she'd taken her mother's advice about visiting the abandoned ghost town. An old copper town, they'd said. Mineshafts everywhere. It had seemed like such an exciting overnight.

But now...

She'd come looking for ghosts, but what she'd found was far, far worse.

He was handing two darts to her and gesturing at the board. "Let's play," he muttered. "*Now.*"

She stared at him, mouth agape.

"I... I don't understand."

"Two shots," he said simply. "You hit the bullseye, you live. What's not to understand?"

"W-why?"

"You can ask, but you may never know. Now, stop stalling."

She tried to think of what to do. Her mind was racing wildly. She wanted to throw the darts at him again, but it had only seemed to enrage the man.

So, with much trembling and terror, she shot quick, hesitant glances towards him as she reluctantly turned to face the old, dusty dartboard.

She didn't play darts.

Two shots to hit a bullseye? It seemed impossible.

"Ready?" he said. "Have at it, girlie."

She let out a faint whimper again, still gripping the dart. Terror flooded her system. And her hand was trembling so badly as she raised it, she nearly dropped the small, fletched projectile.

Swallowing her fear, she gritted her teeth and closed her eyes. Taking a deep breath, she threw the dart at the board with all the strength she could muster.

The dart thudded into the board, a full foot away from the red bullseye. At least she'd hit the board. She hadn't been sure she would.

He scoffed. "Nice try."

She gulped but refused to look at him. She still had one shot left. Closing her eyes, she calmed her breathing. She raised the second dart and took aim.

Time seemed to slow. All the terror and panic she had been feeling culminated as she focused on the bullseye before her. In her mind, she could see it—the path the dart needed to take, the exact trajectory required to hit the target. Clear as day.

She let the dart fly.

A split second later, it embedded itself just below the board, missing it completely.

Silence filled the cellar. He stood motionless, staring at the dart impaled in the wall. She held her breath, feeling as if her legs would give out.

Finally, he stepped back and turned towards her.

The corner of his lip quirked into a small smile. Wordlessly, he gave her a nod. "Been a pleasure," he said simply. "Unlucky."

And then his knife raised and lunged at her.

She didn't even have time to scream.

Chapter 1

Ella gripped the steering wheel of her sedan, knuckles turning white against the cold, as the echo of that threatening phone call flashed through her mind again.

"You want to see him alive again? Come to us. No cops... I'm texting the address. Come right now. Or I'll cut him to pieces and mail them to you."

The man on the phone, one of two assassins sent after her by the Collective, was talking about her boyfriend, Brenner Gunn.

Her heart raced. Brenner was the only person left that she cared about in this godforsaken tundra. She had to get to him. Now.

The snow whipped against the windshield as Ella accelerated down the icy road, barely able to see five feet in front of her. Her tires skidded and fishtailed with every turn. The heater strained against the chill seeping through the cracks and crevices of the sedan.

This blizzard was picking back up again, spattering crystals against her windshield. But Ella couldn't wait. She had to get to Brenner.

"Dammit," she muttered through gritted teeth as she wrestled with the steering wheel. Her knuckles burned from clenching so hard.

The sedan groaned under the strain of fighting through nearly a half-foot of fresh snow that had managed to escape the patrol of diggers-turned-plows.

Ella's heart pounded in time with the wind rattling the roof of the car. She blinked away the snowflakes clinging to her eyelashes, coming through the window she'd rolled down to aid in visibility. She peered ahead, barely making out the turnoff for Brenner's road in the whirling whiteness.

If anything happened to him...

If he was killed because of *her*...

What were they doing to him right now? At this very moment?

Ella turned onto Brenner's road, fishtailing for a moment before regaining control of the sedan. The familiar path was now completely obscured, but it didn't matter. She knew this road by heart. She'd find her way to Brenner if she had to drive blind.

She rounded the final bend and slammed on the brakes, skidding to a stop.

Black smoke billowed into the sky, stark against the pale gray clouds. An acrid stench filled the air, choking and bitter. The smell of burning plastic and wood.

Ella threw open the car door and stumbled out into the knee-deep snow. Her boots sank into the drifts as she trudged toward the source of the smoke.

Brenner's apartment.

Flames leapt from the windows, three floors up, orange tongues licking at the weathered walls, eaten at by the saline breeze from the Bering Sea. Most of the structure remained untouched, but the flames jetted out of the window to Brenner's unit.

Figures were fleeing the front doors. A crying child was looking for his mother.

Ella's heart lodged in her throat. "Brenner!" she screamed, trying to run through the snow. She slipped and stumbled, struggling to stay on her feet.

She had to get inside. She had to find him. He couldn't be gone. Not like this.

Ella finally reached the front door and grabbed the handle, yanking it open. She nearly slammed into a man wearing only boxers sprinting out into the snow. Smoke billowed down the stairwell, and her heart pounded horribly.

She rounded the banister, once, twice. Trying to keep low, trying not to inhale the smoke.

She reached the third floor. A blast of scorching heat sent her reeling back, flames erupting from the doorway.

She shielded her face with an arm, squinting against the inferno. "Brenner!" she shouted again. There, through the flames, a dark shape on the floor. A body.

But it was so damn hot.

She couldn't wait. But couldn't lunge in. Even if she did, she wouldn't be able to drag Brenner out without burning him.

So...

Her mind whirred, moving fast. Her thoughts a blur.

And then she spotted it. The unit across the hall. One of the neighbors had left their door wide open in the urgency to flee.

Her eyes widened.

She sprinted towards this open door, moving faster than one might've thought possible.

It felt like pulling her own teeth to turn her back on Brenner and run in the opposite direction, but she had a plan.

She charged into the open apartment unit, stumbled into a small bathroom, as the layout was similar enough to Brenner's, and jumped into the shower.

Fully clothed, she turned on the cold water, spraying herself.

Her mind flickered back to another memory.

A shower... this time back in Brenner's, with him. The two of them wrapped in each other's arms.

"Dammit! Come on!" she yelled at the blast of cold water.

It soaked her. Pouring down her face, her clothing. She grabbed a towel from the rack and soaked this as well.

Then she sprinted out the door, towel and all, dripping water, soaked and wet, her body covered in a layer of frigid water. For once, she felt a surge of gratitude for how cold Nome's water tanks could get.

She held the towel up to her face and body, protecting herself from the smoke and heat as she stumbled towards Brenner's apartment door. No sirens in the distance. She couldn't hear them.

Where the hell were the cops?

Some had come to help her apprehend a killer, but most should have been responding by now, with the fire trucks... Where were they?

These thoughts churned through her mind but didn't last.

Summoning every ounce of her courage, Ella plunged into the raging fire.

The heat was unbearable and would've seared Ella's skin if not for the water which was now steaming off her in plumes. She dropped to the floor, crawling below the worst of the smoke. Her eyes streamed and her throat burned with every breath.

"Brenner!" She shook his shoulder, barely able to see through the haze. He was unconscious but alive—she could feel the shallow rise and fall of his chest.

The floorboards groaned overhead. Flaming debris crashed down around them, embers scattering across the floor. The unit was coming down.

They had to get out. Now.

Ella looped Brenner's arm over her shoulders and dragged him toward the doorway, ignoring the flames licking at her clothes.

But he was twice her size.

This wasn't like the movies. She cursed as she tried to drag him, wrapping her soaked towel around his face and arms. Step by agonizing step, they inched forward. But they couldn't reach the door.

He was too damn heavy, and the fire had spread.

She cursed, glancing around in the swirling smoke.

Again, her mind was moving at a rapid pace.

She reached a decision.

"Brenner! Brenner, wake up!" She slapped at him. She couldn't carry him, she just needed some help. Only a little—

He let out a wheezing gasp, choking.

Alive.

She felt a burst of relief. But it was short-lived. They were both going to be burned alive if she didn't hurry.

She dragged Brenner up, and in his groggy, disoriented state, he helped by stumbling along and letting her guide him.

Towards the window.

"Hold on!" she yelled.

The blizzard was going to save them. It would have to.

The freshly fallen snow was the only soft landing they had.

She shoved Brenner forward, the two of them picking up speed as Brenner tried to gather his wits.

"Come on!" she yelled. "Jump!"

They slammed into the glass.

It shattered around them as the two of them jumped from the third-floor apartment unit, leaping in a column of smoke, out into the frigid, arctic air.

They hit a thick bank of snow under the window, where plows had pushed it from the street.

Ella slammed into the snow, cutting straight through it. She hit the ground with a *thump*. And she lay there, trembling, equal parts freezing and warm.

She let out a wheezing gasp.

She tested her arms. Her legs.

Bruised. Not broken.

Her cheeks stung from the cold. With a groan, she pushed to her feet, rising from the crater in the snow.

Brenner was also rising like some zombie, wincing and hacking.

When they finally stumbled out from the snowbank, Ella's vision swam. Her legs gave out from under her and she collapsed, Brenner sprawled next to her.

She lay there, gazing up at the sky. The thick black smoke was receding now, whipped away by the wind. In its place, a pale circle of light peered through. The sun—or maybe the moon. Ella couldn't tell anymore.

All she knew was that they'd made it out. They were alive. Brenner was safe.

As the snowflakes continued to fall, Ella let her eyes drift shut. They had survived the fire. The rest could wait until morning.

A small, niggling worry wormed into her mind, though.

The two assassins had come for Brenner. Had stolen his phone. Left him alive...

And then?

Just fled?

She lay there, frowning briefly.

There was a phrase her father often used when he'd go hunting with Dr. Messer, the local coroner.

Smoke 'em out.

To smoke a wild creature from its hiding spot, by setting something ablaze to lure it into the open. Providing the hunters a clear shot.

She frowned, considering this, propping up on one arm.

And it was as she moved that she heard the gunshot.

A whirring *whizzing* sound, and then the snow *directly* under where her head had been seconds before, exploded in a burst of ice.

Instinctively, she began moving again.

"Sniper!" she yelled.

Brenner was blinking, the cold of the snow and ice having seemingly roused him. He was groggy, though. Drugged?

She shoved at him, sending him stumbling back into the snowbank as there was another loud *crack*! Coming from the direction of a large work crane over the nearest dock.

She thought she spotted a muzzle flash.

She was now moving again. The neighbors had scattered. Still no sign of sirens. No sound of first responders.

Where the hell were they?

She grabbed at Brenner's arm as twin gunshots resounded simultaneously. Two shooters.

This time, a car mirror exploded by her right hand as she pulled Brenner down next to her, taking cover behind the car.

Another shot. Sparks erupted off the hood of the car, raining down on them.

"Shit," Brenner was muttering, still blinking blearily, clearly trying to catch his bearings.

Another gunshot echoed through the stillness. A glass window behind them exploded.

Brenner ducked instinctively, but now he seemed to be regaining his senses.

His arms had superficial burns on them. His body was trembling from the cold, but he ignored all of it.

Instead, he reached out, snapping off the car mirror above him.

"What are you doing?" she hissed.

He shook his head, holding a finger to his lips.

She watched as Brenner angled the mirror, reflecting back in the direction of the sniper.

Another shot.

"They've got us pinned down," Brenner said, cursing. "Two shooters. Covering both egress points on the street. Building is going to come down soon." He rattled it all off matter-of-factly as if he were narrating the news.

"So what should we do?" Ella whispered. Her lungs still ached and her throat felt as if she'd swallowed a tablet of acid.

Brenner frowned, deep in thought, and then he smashed his elbow through the car window.

"What are you doing?"

"We gotta move. So our cover has to also."

The car was already shot to pieces. It wasn't either of theirs, and Ella had no clue how to hot-wire a vehicle like this.

But Brenner wasn't trying anything so fancy.

Instead, he pushed the parking brake and put the car in neutral.

The alarm started blaring. The single, remaining headlight flashing. But Brenner didn't slow, even with the shrill squeal echoing around them.

He shoved his shoulder into the open door, and with Ella's help, he began to push the car down the street, using it for cover, moving the car with them as they crouched behind it.

More gunshots echoed. A dent appeared in the roof, just above Ella's head. She winced, imagining that not much would be left if one of those bullets struck her.

They literally had a moving target. The moving car not only offered Brenner and Ella cover but also provided them with a means of making progress towards safety. Brenner gritted his teeth, pushing harder as they both rounded the corner, the car's alarm still blaring.

Ella felt like they had been pushing the car forever. Her palms were sweaty despite the cold, and her legs were shaking beneath her. Suddenly, they heard the sound of an engine behind them, and without warning, Brenner ducked, pulling Ella down with him.

A sleek black SUV flew past them, its side window rolled down.

Blue lights flashed from the windshield.

A cop car.

Ella now heard sirens.

The cavalry had finally arrived, but what had caused the delay?

She glanced towards the crane by the docks where the snipers had been perched, but it looked as if they were now fleeing, judging by two small, black blurs moving along a service ladder.

No more gunshots.

More sirens as more cop cars hastened towards them.

Ella released a small gasp of relief as she collapsed.

She closed her eyes briefly. "Holy crap," she whispered. "Are you okay?"

Brenner was wheezing badly, wincing as he glanced at the shallow burns on his arm, but he flashed a thumbs up.

"Thanks," he whispered. "You saved me."

"Returning the favor," she shot back.

He nodded, leaning his head against hers where they crouched side by side in the cover of their dented bullet shield.

His head felt sweat-slicked where he leaned against her, but she didn't draw back.

She turned, glancing towards an approaching ambulance. She raised her hands, waving it down.

"Hey! Hey, we need help! Now!"

The ambulance veered off, moving towards them now. Brenner was now putting snow on his arms, wincing as he did.

Ella found she could breathe easier as the puffs of air arose from her lips like gusts of steam.

Why had the cops come so late?

She could see strained looks on the faces of the men now surging from the first vehicle to reach the burning building.

She could see the frantic nature of their movements. The fear.

Something else had happened.

Something she didn't know about.

And even as this thought occurred to her, and as the paramedics raced over from the ambulance she'd flagged...

Her phone began to ring.

Chapter 2

Ella burst into the Nome police station, the doors slamming behind her in the frigid, Alaskan air. Chaos reigned everywhere.

Three police officers nearly slammed into her as they moved back out into the parking lot.

Two more were yelling something at the desk attendant.

A group of ten looked as if they were discussing something serious by a white-board in the conference hall.

Ella's fingers kept tapping against her phone as she moved hastily forward. The call had brought clarity. It made sense, now, why the first responders had all been busy.

"Holy..." she muttered under her breath. "The Governor's daughter?"

Her breath came out in puffs as she scanned the room, a cacophony of ringing phones and murmured conversations. The atmosphere was electric, charged with anticipation.

She paused suddenly, frowning across the room towards the group of ten.

Ella spotted her twin sister standing beside Chief Baker, her husband. Priscilla's face mirrored the severity of her tailored suit—all sharp angles and dark lines.

Priscilla was glaring directly at Ella.

Ella tried to glance away if only to spare herself the awkward conversation, but Priscilla was the far more direct of the two.

The pretty, blonde-haired woman with the upturned, celestial nose and blue-gray eyes glared at her sister, raised a hand, and gestured wildly like a trainer calling a hound to heel.

"Where have you been?" Priscilla snapped, not bothering to hide her irritation. Ella met her sister's demanding gaze. The tension between them crackled, a storm brewing just beneath the surface.

"Got here as fast as I could," Ella replied defensively, feeling the familiar sting of resentment. She decided to completely skip the events back at Brenner's apartment. Eventually, one of Baker's lackeys would fill them in, but Ella wasn't in a volunteering mood.

The other gathered officers were still watching as Baker droned on, updating them on road-clearing. But every now and then, the boys and girls in blue glanced out of the corners of their eyes at the two twins from Nome.

"What's going on?" Ella said, coming to a halt only a few paces from Cilla. "The dispatch said it was about the governor's daughter?"

"Yes," snapped Cilla. "And we need every able body on this case." Priscilla folded her arms across her chest. She wasn't a cop, but she had a way of making her presence known, barking orders as if she held a badge herself.

"Priscilla, why don't you handle the rest of this—you were on the phone with dispatch," Chief Baker interjected, stepping forward to guide Ella away from her sister. His voice was calm, yet firm—an anchor amidst the chaos. He was used to leadership—he'd been the high school quarterback back in the day after all. His large hands pushed at the small of her back, guiding her away from her sister and into an office at his side.

He then swiveled, turning to her. The sounds from outside were more muffled now. But his features were stretched in worry. "We need federal cooperation on this, Ella," he said quickly. "That's why I had you called in. What can you get me?"

"Get you?"

He nodded fiercely. "She was taken from Nome. The blizzard is keeping the cops out from Juneau. The governor has called twice."

Baker's face had gone pale now, and he swallowed. She made the *gulp* sound for him in her mind.

"We've got a high-profile missing girl on our hands, Ella. Lila Hunt."

The governor's daughter.

"Alright..." Ella muttered under her breath, her heart tightening in her chest. "What happened?"

"Taken from her school earlier today," Chief Baker explained, his brow furrowing as he handed her a file overflowing with papers and photographs. "We're redirecting most of our forces there for the search. We need your help, Ella. Anything the Feds can provide."

"You know we don't have much of a field office here, Baker. Not sure what you expect me to do." Her fingers gripped the edges of the folder.

He glanced urgently through the door, gnawing on his lip and shaking his head in frustration. Priscilla's echoing voice could be heard over the sound of scurrying footsteps and distant sirens.

Ella stifled a yawn, holding a hand to her lips.

Her brother-in-law caught her hand.

The broad-shouldered ex-athlete had grown out his mustache. He wore a large, brass belt buckle and large boots with jeans, giving him the look of a rancher rather than the chief of police. His hands were rough, calloused where they gripped her wrist.

"What's this?" he demanded.

She pulled her hand back, realizing, flushed, he was staring at a burn mark along her fingers.

"Nothing," she said.

"Where were you after we collared that killer?"

Ella just shook her head. She didn't want to get into it. Questions about Brenner's apartment would lead to questions about the assassins. The Collective.

Baker hesitated. "You hear there was a shooting on Straight street?"

"Hmm?"

"Couple of riflemen shooting up a car. Haven't seen the report yet," he said slowly, eyes narrowed. "But that's near that marshal's place, isn't it?"

"Brenner?" she said, innocently. At the mention of her boyfriend's name, she felt a jolt of regret.

She wished he could've been there with her, but Brenner's burns would require twenty-four hours of supervision.

Ella moved quickly on from the subject. The *Collective* had gone after her father. Had gone after Brenner.

There was no telling who they'd target next.

And as she stood there, she couldn't help but remember her father's demand.

A trade.

He had helped her, and now it was her job to find the Architect, the eccentric billionaire who funded a secret society of serial killers.

If anyone could help her locate someone like that, it would be the governor's office.

She winced as she thought it, inwardly chastising herself. It was the sort of thing Priscilla would think of. Opportunistic to the max.

She shook her head, trying to refocus.

"What do we know about the abduction?"

"Still piecing it together," he sighed, rubbing the back of his neck. "But we need to act fast before this turns into a full-blown media circus."

Ella nodded, understanding the urgency of the situation. It was late, but her adrenaline was high. Someone was targeting her family. She hesitated. "I need you to put some uniforms on the hospital," she said simply.

"What?"

"You heard me."

"I can't spare it," he said.

She met his gaze, her eyes like ice. "Then I'm not sure how much I'll be able to help, either."

He stared at her, but she didn't look away.

"Fine," he muttered. "I can spare two."

"Six, at least," she demanded. "And get hospital security armed."

"Four," he retorted. "Final offer."

She sighed, picturing Brenner in the burn ward. If the assassins went after him a second time, she wanted to make sure he'd have backup. She'd already helped smuggle his service weapon under his bed.

One could never be too safe.

She glanced through the door now, looking at Cilla.

As much as she hated to admit it, and as much as she wanted to take the night off, get some sleep, she couldn't shake the obvious conclusion...

Her sister would be a target for these killers.

They'd come after her parents, her boyfriend... her twin would be next, eventually.

Ella sighed.

Besides, opportunistic or not, helping the governor and getting his help in tracking the Collective would change everything.

That way, she could hunt *them* instead of the other way around.

Besides...

Someone had kidnapped a teenager from school.

She frowned, hating how long it had taken her sleep-addled brain and exhausted body to start feeling the rising sense of indignation.

"Alright," she said, determination setting in. "Let's get to work. You said it started at school?"

"Yeah. That's where she was last seen."

"But we don't know if it was the kidnapping site?"

"Working theory."

"Alright. I'll check out the school, but Baker, I mean it... Four cops. At the hospital, like five minutes ago."

"Fine," he said, raising both hands. "Fine. Deal."

She nodded and with a final nod to Chief Baker, Ella stepped out of the room and moved back towards the sliding glass doors, the urgency of the situation fueling her every step.

She could only hope she could find something to locate Lila Hunt... before it was all too late.

Chapter 3

The drive to Lila Hunt's school was a blur, Ella's thoughts consumed by the details of the abduction.

As she pulled up to the school, a somber sight greeted her: students filed out in orderly lines, their faces etched with confusion and sadness. A heavy silence hung over the scene, punctuated only by the occasional sniffle or hushed whisper. The school, usually a bustling hive of activity, now seemed more like a hastily abandoned ghost town.

Inside, the remaining students were corralled into the cafeteria, the smell of uneaten lunches still lingering in the air. Ella noticed a group of teenagers huddled together near the back, currently being watched by a couple of plainclothes officers—the children were likely friends of Lila. Ella began to make her way toward them. The fluorescent lights above cast a harsh glow, etching deep shadows on their solemn faces.

One of the plainclothes spotted her and moved to intercept.

"Agent Porter," the bearded man said, recognizing her. He adjusted his glasses and rubbed one lens on his sleeve.

"Hey Mike, those the witnesses?"

"Not witnesses," he corrected. "But friends of Lila."

Ella pressed her lips together. "Mind if I speak with 'em?"

"Baker know?"

"Baker sent me."

"Right. Whatever you need, agent."

Something about the cop's attitude, his demeanor communicated the same level of concern she'd seen back at the station.

It was late, and the children had been held at the school during the blizzard. She checked her watch. Nearly eight PM.

"They've held them here for four hours?" she asked in a hushed voice.

The cop nodded. "Roads were closed." A shrug. "Snow," he said by way of explanation.

She frowned, glancing at the weary faces of the children, which matched her own. The double shot of espresso on the way over had somewhat helped her, and the bandage she had over the burn marks on her hand had assuaged some of her discomfort.

Now she approached the children seated at the lunch table, moving carefully forward as if she were afraid she might spook them.

"Excuse me," Ella said softly as she approached the group. Their heads snapped up, eyes wide with a mixture of fear and curiosity. "I'm Agent Porter. I hear you guys have been here a while."

Blank stares.

"I'm sorry about that. Your parents all know where you are, and I promise to get you out of here as soon as possible. Are you guys hungry? Thirsty?"

"I could eat," a boy piped up, leaning back and crossing his arms under a dangling chain.

Ella acknowledged him with a nod, glancing towards a vending machine across the cafeteria. She pulled a few dollar bills from her wallet and handed them to him.

He grinned and hopped to his feet, moving quickly towards the vending machine.

She returned her attention to the others.

"Mind if I ask a few questions about your friend?" she said in that same even, gentle voice.

The two plainclothes babysitters looked relieved that she'd shown up and had retreated from the group of high schoolers.

The boy with the chain returned with three bags of chips and a chocolate bar. He tossed the chocolate bar to a girl sitting in the back of the group.

Ella blinked, doing a double take. She stared at the young girl in the back who had earbuds in and was listening to music, her eyes closed. She held the chocolate bar in one hand. The girl had blonde hair and the same blue eyes as the Porter sisters. She was quite pretty, though she didn't wear makeup, and her foot kept tapping in rhythm to the music she was listening too.

Despite the weather, the girl was wearing sandals, boldly displaying a foot that only had four toes. One had been amputated more than a month ago, due to frostbite.

Ella stared in surprise at her eighteen-year-old cousin, Maddie Porter. Ella's surprise gave way to concern—what was Maddie doing here?

School.

She realized this was Maddie's school.

Maddie finally opened her eyes, looking up from where she'd been lost in the music. She spotted Ella and stiffened.

Ella waved back.

Maddie's face creased into a wide grin, and she pulled her earbuds from her ear.

"Ella!" she exclaimed. "Hi!" she said, cheerful and bubbly, waving a hand rapidly.

"M-maddie," Ella said cautiously.

Her cousin was now on her feet, taking a bite of the chocolate bar as she approached. She affectionately flicked the ear of the spiky-haired boy who'd brought her the treat.

"Can we chat?" Maddie asked in her same energetic voice, as if she were used to being held after school for hours.

Ella knew that Maddie's home life wasn't exactly ideal. The girl's mother wasn't with them, and her father had health issues, leaving the brunt of caretaking responsibilities on the teenage girl's shoulders.

As Maddie drew closer, she glanced at the two plainclothes cops then back at her cousin.

She seemed to slowly register that this wasn't a social call, as if she'd been lost in the music she'd been listening to and was now allowing her thoughts to slowly seep back into reality.

"Hi, Ella," Maddie offered, her voice barely audible. She gestured for Ella to step aside, away from the others. "Can we talk privately?"

"Of course," Ella agreed, trying to mask her worry. She led her cousin to a quiet corner, away from prying ears. "What's going on, Maddie? I didn't know you knew the governor's daughter."

"I—" Maddie hesitated, her eyes darting back to the group of friends. "We were friends, sort of. I just wanted to tell you that... she wasn't exactly well-liked by everyone."

Ella hesitated. "What do you mean? I thought this was a group of her friends."

"It is," Maddie said quickly, nibbling on the corner of her lip. "But..."

Maddie's voice trailed off, and Ella leaned in to hear her better. Maddie took a deep breath before continuing.

"Lila was involved with some of the wrong people," Maddie whispered, her eyes darting around the room. "I don't know what they were into exactly, but I heard rumors. And I know for a fact she owes some money to some pretty dangerous people." Anticipating the follow-up question, she quickly added, "I don't know who. That's just the rumor going around."

Ella's heart quickened as she listened. This was exactly the kind of information she'd been hoping for. "Do you know anything about who these people are?"

Maddie shook her head. "No, I don't. But I overheard Lila talking about them on the phone. She was scared, Ella. Really scared."

Ella's mind was racing. She thought of her own altercation with threats over the phone. "Thank you, Maddie," she said, placing a hand on her cousin's shoulder. "You've been a big help."

Maddie nodded, a look of relief washing over her face. "Is there anything else I can do?"

Ella hesitated, then shook her head. "No, that's all for now. Just stay safe, okay?"

Maddie nodded again, then turned and walked back towards her friends. Ella watched her go, her mind still whirling with the new information. As she made her way back over to the plainclothes officers, she couldn't help but feel a sense of unease. If Lila was involved with dangerous people, that widened the list of suspects but also narrowed her field of view.

Maybe one of the other kids would know *who* the trouble was with.

She approached the table again, nodding at the kid with the spiky hair and chain. He was munching on chips and licking nacho dust off his fingers.

"Hey," she said, "What's your name?"

He looked up at her, the teenager quirking an eyebrow. He studied her for a moment, projecting indifference to her badge. Ella understood now why this kid seemed to like Maddie.

Peas in a pod. But Maddie's anti-authoritarian streak was of a friendlier variety, with far less jutting chin.

The spiky-haired kid hadn't yet mastered the art of subtlety, it seemed.

She didn't mind. She remembered high school.

"Doug," he said simply.

The six others at the table all glanced at him, then back at her, as if they were watching a tennis match.

"Hey Doug," Ella said quietly. "You were a friend of Lila's?"

Doug's expression hardened. He took another handful of chips, chewing thoughtfully. "Yeah," he finally said, the word slow and deliberate. "We knew each other. Not like we were best friends or anything."

"Did she ever mention anything about owing money to anyone?" Ella asked, her voice betraying nothing. She didn't glance in Maddie's direction.

The group around the table tensed, their faces looking like they had been suddenly painted with a mask. Silence fell over the group for a moment, and then one of the girls finally spoke. A girl wearing twice as much makeup as usual, as if to make up for Maddie's aversion.

"I heard her talking about it on the phone with someone," this girl said slowly. Part of her mascara was streaked as if she'd been crying. "Lila was scared. Really scared."

Ella's heart quickened. It seemed that Maddie wasn't the only one who had overheard Lila discussing her money troubles.

"Do you have any idea who she might have been in trouble with?" Ella asked, trying not to appear too pushy.

The group exchanged glances as if deciding whether or not to disclose what they knew. Finally, the boy sitting next to Doug spoke up.

"I heard her mention something about the Clyde brothers," he said, his voice barely audible. "But I don't know anything else."

Ella's blood ran cold at the mention of the Clyde Brothers. They ran an antique wood-working store in the heart of Nome, but everyone knew it was just a front. Most of the sordid things found in Nome would pass through the Clyde brothers. Prostitution, gambling, illegal dog fights. They toed the line. Rarely going so far over it that they incurred Chief Baker's wrath, but they played fast and loose with the rules. If Lila, a teenage girl, was really mixed up with them, then she was in more danger than Ella had previously thought.

"Who saw Lila last, before school let out?" Ella asked.

The group looked at each other, unsure of what to say. Finally, Doug spoke up. "I saw her leaving with some guy. Didn't recognize him."

A couple of the others shot looks at him as if this were the first time they were hearing it.

Ella's eyes narrowed. "Can you describe him?"

Doug shook his head. "Sorry, I didn't get a good look. But he was tall, skinny, and had a buzz cut. That's all I remember."

Ella jotted down the description in her notebook, then looked back up at the group. "Thank you for your help," she said, her voice softening. "I know this must be tough for you guys."

The group murmured their thanks then quickly returned to their snacks and conversation as if trying to erase the tense moment that had just occurred. Ella took a deep breath, then turned on her heel and strode over to one of the plainclothes officers.

She couldn't shake the feeling that she was getting closer to the truth, but also that Lila Hunt was in over her head. The Clyde brothers were no joke, and if they were involved with Lila's disappearance, then she needed to tread carefully.

Ella watched as the other officer waved at the group of students, gesturing for them to file towards the door.

Maddie gave her cousin a quick wave and a smile. Ella returned it.

As the students filed out of the cafeteria, Ella couldn't shake the feeling that she was missing something important. That's when she noticed it—a subtle exchange between two of the students, a folded note surreptitiously changing hands. One of the other boys slipping something to Doug.

The kid with the Dorito dust on his fingers accepted the note, leaving an orange streak before slipping it into his pocket.

Ella stopped the plainclothes officer mid-sentence.

"I mean, we could double check with," he was saying.

But she turned and began moving after the students, frowning. She felt instinct drawing her after them.

Ella threaded her way through the cafeteria, her eyes locked onto the backs of the two students who had exchanged the note. Their quiet muttering mingled with the cacophony of voices and footsteps echoing through the school's hallway.

"So what's that about?" she muttered, her voice barely audible over the din.

As Ella rounded the corner, she caught sight of the two students slipping through a door at the end of the hall. The fluorescent lights overhead flickered ominously, casting eerie shadows that danced along the walls.

The door creaked open as Ella approached, revealing a darkened stairwell leading down into the bowels of the school. A chill ran down her spine, and she hesitated for just a moment before descending into the darkness.

There was no further sound, save for the distant echo of hurried footsteps. Ella cursed under her breath as she moved down the stairs, her hand gripping the railing for support in the dim light. With every step, the air grew colder, heavier—suffocating her with its weight.

At the bottom of the staircase, Ella found herself facing a long, narrow corridor lined with lockers and doors. She glanced around, her eyes struggling to adjust to the darkness. The silence was deafening, broken only by the distant hum of the school's heating system.

A door creaked open at the far end of the corridor, and for a moment, Ella caught sight of a figure slipping through it.

As she reached the door, Ella hesitated once more, her hand hovering over the cold metal handle. Anticipation mixed with determination as she steeled herself, pushing aside her doubts.

With one final deep breath, Ella gripped the handle and pulled the door open. The hinges creaked ominously, like low groans in a graveyard. Shivers trembled down her spine as she stepped into the room beyond.

Chapter 4

The musty scent of damp concrete assaulted Ella's senses as she descended the creaky wooden stairs into the dark basement. The dim glow of her flashlight barely pierced the heavy shadows, revealing dust-coated furniture and yellowed newspapers piled high on sagging shelves. She frowned, staring down the stairs.

There was no sign of the two students. No sign of Doug with his spiky hair and swaying, faux-silver chain.

But as she took the stairs, she heard a distant thud followed by muffled whispers. Sweat trickled down her brow as she moved deeper into the gloom, her flashlight beam bouncing off the walls like a timid intruder. Obstacles littered her path; discarded boxes, rusty bicycles, and broken appliances lay strewn across the cold concrete floor.

"Damn it," she muttered under her breath as she stumbled over an old sewing machine, her leg protesting at the impact. But she couldn't let anything deter her now; she needed answers. It looked as if an arts and crafts class had been using this space, or perhaps just dumping their trash down here.

Her determination fueled her onward, navigating the labyrinth of forgotten relics. She squinted as her flashlight flickered, cursing the cheap batteries she'd bought from the gas station. Ella shook the device, coaxing a stronger beam of light from it.

"Come on, don't fail me now," she whispered, feeling a shiver run down her spine as the whispers grew louder. A sense of foreboding tightened around her chest, but she pushed it aside, reminding herself why she was here—Lila Hunt, the governor's daughter, the girl who had vanished. Involved with the Clyde Brothers, apparently. And not particularly liked, according to Maddie.

She turned off her flashlight beam now, as the path turned into a hall, leading towards a flickering light at the end of the space. The whispers were coming from the far room.

The steady dripping of water echoed through the basement, and Ella inched to the doorway, her shoulder pressing against cold, unfinished concrete. Her gaze finally landed on two teenage boys—one tall and lanky with an unruly mop of hair, the other shorter and stockier with the chain. It was Doug and his friend, both of them red-faced and straining as they attempted to maneuver a large, bulky object from beneath a rusted water heater.

"Got it... almost," Doug grunted, sweat beading on his forehead. "Pick up your side, asshole."

"I am! It's not moving."

"Hey!" she called out, her voice authoritative and commanding. Both boys jumped, their heads whipping around to face her. "What the hell are you doing down here?" Doug said, instinctively.

The taller boy gaped, fear flashing across his face. Ella could sense their guilt.

"What are you two doing down here?" she said slowly, brandishing her badge, her eyes never leaving them.

"Uh, we were just..." Doug started, glancing nervously at his companion, who shot him a warning look.

As Ella's gaze bore into the teenagers, Doug's friend shifted his weight uneasily from one foot to the other, his eyes darting around the dimly lit basement. Sweat trickled down the side of his face, glistening in the faint light cast by a single, bare bulb hanging overhead. His hands clenched and unclenched, the tension palpable.

"Look," Doug stammered, his voice barely more than a whisper, "we don't want any trouble." As he spoke, his friend surreptitiously inched toward a rusty water pipe lying on the floor, evidently hoping that Ella wouldn't notice.

"Trouble?" Ella responded icily, her instincts kicking in. "You're already in trouble. Now start talking before this gets worse for you."

Doug's friend lunged for the water pipe, grasping it tightly in his trembling hands as he swung it wildly at Ella. But Ella was prepared for the attack; years of training had honed her reflexes, especially against a couple of kids. She sidestepped the clumsy swing with ease, her heart pounding in her chest as adrenaline coursed through her veins.

She seized the teenager's wrist mid-swing, wrenching the pipe from his grasp. With a fluid motion, she twisted his arm behind his back, forcing him to his knees with a grunt of pain.

"Please," Doug pleaded, panic etched across his face as he stared at where his friend knelt, gripped by Ella. "You don't understand. We just... we needed the money."

Ella's grip tightened on the taller teenager's arm, her resolve unwavering. She couldn't afford to let sympathy cloud her judgment. The case was too important. Vaguely, she wondered if the governor was flying in. "It doesn't matter," she said coldly. "You've made your choices, and now you have to face the consequences."

"Please," Doug's friend whimpered as Ella maintained her hold on him. "We'll tell you everything. Just... don't hurt us."

Ella hesitated for a moment, her mind racing as she considered her options. Letting them go was out of the question, but she knew that their cooperation would be crucial in unraveling the opacity surrounding Lila Hunt's disappearance. Finally, she released her grip on the teenager's arm, watching as he cradled it against his chest with a grimace.

"Alright," she said, her voice steady and commanding. "Talk. And don't even think about lying or holding back information."

But both the teens just stared at each other, wincing and grimacing.

Ella's gaze shifted to the handcuffs hanging from her belt, glinting in the dim light of the basement. Her fingers curled around them with practiced ease as she snapped one end onto Doug's wrist, then guided his struggling friend to sit next to him before securing the other cuff on his friend's wrist. The metallic click echoed through the room, reinforcing the gravity of their situation.

"Stay put," Ella warned, her ice-cold tone leaving no room for argument. She turned her attention back to the water heater, curiosity gnawing at her like a starving animal. What could possibly be so important that these two would risk everything to protect it?

"Wh-what are you gonna do to us?" stammered Doug's friend, his voice shaking with fear.

"Depends on what I find," Ella replied without taking her eyes off the water heater. She crouched down, examining the large object the teenagers had been trying to remove. Carefully, she gripped its edges, muscles tensing as she dragged it out from under the appliance.

The moment the object was exposed, Ella's heart skipped a beat. Inside a torn plastic bag lay a multitude of brightly colored pills, their sinister appearance belying the sense of euphoria they promised. Ecstasy.

"Nice..." Ella muttered under her breath, her mind racing with the implications of this discovery. According to Maddie, Lila owed a bunch of money to certain folk. She had connections to the Clyde Brothers' outfit. She stared at the pills, pieces falling into place.

"Where'd you get this?" Ella demanded, holding up the bag for them to see.

"Th-they just gave it to us!" Doug stammered, his face pale. "They said we just had to sell it and deliver the money."

"Who's 'they'?" Ella asked, her patience wearing thin.

Doug hesitated, his eyes darting between Ella and his friend. Finally, he exhaled a shaky breath, saying, "I don't know their names, but they're dangerous people, alright? We didn't have a choice."

"Everyone has a choice," Ella countered, her grip on the bag of ecstasy tightening. She couldn't help but feel a pang of sympathy for the two boys, but she also knew their involvement in this drug operation was too closely tied to the governor's daughter's disappearance.

"Please," Doug whispered, his voice trembling. "We didn't want any of this."

The dim light from the single, dust-covered bulb hanging above them cast eerie shadows on the basement walls. Ella stood over the hand-cuffed teenagers as they huddled together on the cold, damp floor, their frightened breaths echoing throughout the confined space. Doug's friend, the lanky kid with unkempt hair, stared wide-eyed at her, his body shivering uncontrollably. Doug looked calmer, though, the fear in his eyes was unmistakable.

"Alright," Ella began, focusing her gaze on Doug. "You're going to tell me everything you know about Lila Hunt's involvement in this, and you're not leaving anything out. Understood?"

Doug swallowed hard, sweat beading on his forehead as he glanced at his friend for reassurance. He nodded hesitantly. "Y-yeah, I understand."

"Good. Now start talking," she said, her voice firm, yet carefully controlled, giving no room for argument.

Doug took a deep breath and closed his eyes briefly before opening them again as if gathering strength from within. "Lila... she was one of our dealers. She came to us a few months ago, said she needed some extra cash. And since we went to the same school, it seemed like a good idea, y'know?"

"Did she ever mention any names?" Ella asked, her mind racing with questions and potential leads.

"Names? Like buyers? No," Doug replied, shaking his head. "She just picked up the stuff from us and gave us the money later. We never asked questions."

"Did she have any connection to the people who supplied you with the drugs?" Ella questioned further, her persistence unyielding.

"Uhm, I don't think so," Doug answered hesitantly, his gaze flickering between Ella and his friend. "I mean, we never met our suppliers either. Everything was all... anonymous, I guess."

"Anonymous," Ella repeated, her frustration mounting as she curled the fingers on her left hand over her palm.

"Did anything happen recently that might have led to her disappearance? Did she say or do anything out of the ordinary?" she continued, her voice urgent as she sought any scrap of information that could help her piece together the puzzle.

Doug hesitated, his eyes searching the floor as if hoping the answer would materialize before him. "Well... a few days before she disappeared, she mentioned she'd found something out. Something big. But she wouldn't tell us what it was. She just... looked scared."

"Scared?"

"Yeah, like... really scared. Like she knew something bad was going to happen."

Ella sighed, her thoughts racing. The governor's daughter, a drug dealer, scared and holding onto some dangerous secret—it was all starting to feel like all of Nome was going haywire.

She glanced at the two boys.

"Look," Doug said suddenly, "We... we can tell you how to contact our supplier. I have his number. Just—just we can forget about that, right?" He winced, glancing at the pills.

Ella looked at him.

She'd gotten in trouble in the past for letting a criminal go. Then again, Mortimer Graves had saved her life more than once.

She massaged the bridge of her nose. Then, quietly, she said, "I can put in a good word. Maybe cut a deal, but only if you help me find Lila."

The two teens looked sick, both pale. But Doug was nodding so feverishly, his oversized chain rattled.

"So," Ella said firmly, "Is your supplier one of the Clyde Brothers?"

Doug shared a look with his friend. "I told you, we don't know. But I can give you the number we use."

"Deal," Ella said with a simple shrug.

She opened her mouth to speak further, but before she could, her own phone began to ring.

She frowned, glancing down. She answered, "Hey Baker, what's up?"

"Ella?" said her brother-in-law, his voice grim. "You see the notice?"

"What notice?"

"Dammit, Ella. Keep bulletins on."

She just frowned. "What is it, Baker?"

"They found a girl. A body."

Ella felt her heart freeze.

"Not Lila," he said quickly. "Not possible."

She relaxed but still felt a tinge of grief. "But you think it's connected?"

"Wearing the school uniform," he said, still grim. "Body hasn't been identified yet."

"From *this* school? Another victim? Where?"

A long sigh, "That's the thing. She was discovered at the bottom of a mineshaft. In the Kennicott Ghost Town. You know it?"

Ella blinked. She resisted the urge to scratch at her ear as if it might help her hear better. "That's... seven hundred miles away," she said.

"But still in Alaska," he replied. "And like I said, we need federal resources. Can you check it out?"

She held her breath, wincing. But then she said, "I'll get a flight. Tell them not to touch anything."

"That won't be a problem," Baker came back. "They still haven't found a way to get the body out of the mineshaft. Thanks, Ella—Shit. Another call. Governor. Shit. Shit. Shi—"

His last cuss was cut off as he hung up, leaving Ella in silence.

She sighed, turning and gesturing. "Give me that number and come with me," she said brusquely. Normally, she might've been a bit more considerate.

But now, by the sound of things, she had a flight to catch.

Chapter 5

Ella shivered as she stepped from the vehicle that had picked her up from the airport.

She surveyed the row of emergency service vehicles lining the path leading to the foot of the mountain.

Small flashlights swept like lighthouse beams in the dark, and she spotted large construction equipment near a tall building.

Her eyes moved from one building to the next, even as her breath plumed in the air, and she stretched her legs following the four-hour flight. She'd managed to get some sleep in the airplane and on the hour drive from the airport.

Now, she didn't quite feel *well* rested, but she was glad for the new company.

Brenner tugged at her sleeve, frowning down to the valley.

"See anything like that before?"

She shook her head once, then shot him a glance.

She'd asked him to stay behind, but the hospital had released him, most of his superficial burns treated. And he hadn't wanted her out of his sight.

Besides, she'd figured the safest place for Brenner was 700 miles away from Nome, at her side.

She patted him on the back, trying not to stare at the bandage peaking past the edge of his jacket sleeve.

But soon, both of them were staring down at the crime scene below.

The Kennicott Ghost Town in Alaska stood silent as a tomb, its skeletal remains a testament to the once-thriving copper mining community that had long been abandoned. The wind whistled through the decaying buildings, rusted machinery lay scattered like the discarded toys of a giant child, and the mountains rose up behind it all, watching over the desolate scene.

Ella surveyed the town with a mixture of fascination and unease. "Never thought I'd find myself investigating a murder in a place like this," she muttered to herself, her breath fogging up in the frigid Alaskan air. The rising sun only just peeked from behind the mountains, starting to cast the gloomy town into a bronze glow.

As she walked towards the mineshaft where she'd spotted the machinery, she picked up on the faint sound of commotion. Her instincts kicked in, urging her forward, Brenner following close behind. Neither of them wanted too much distance between them. Not now. Not after what they'd endured. Brenner and Ella still hadn't talked about the attack. Brenner hadn't pried, and Ella hadn't volunteered. But they both knew who was responsible and why Ella was being targeted.

Still, she thought to herself, sighing and watching the mist plume, now wasn't the time for *that* conversation.

As Ella approached the elevator mineshaft, like a giant crater in the ground with an old wooden structure as a backstop, she saw a small crowd gathered around the entrance to the mine. She pushed her way through the onlookers, just in time to see a crane lowering a lifeless body to the ground. The metallic groan of the crane's gears pierced the air, matched only by the gasps and hushed whispers of the bystanders.

"Finally got it, huh?" someone murmured behind her. "Just in time for the damn Feds."

"Shhh!" another voice hissed, silencing any further speculation.

Ella's eyes remained fixed on the horrifying sight before her. The victim was a woman, dressed in a simple cotton dress that hung limply off her pale, lifeless frame. She had on a jacket, too… It carried the bulldog emblem from Maddie's high school. What was a student from Nome doing all the way out here? And was it a harbinger of things to come in the governor's daughter's case?

"Agent, we didn't touch anything," a uniformed officer whispered to her, noticing her intense gaze. "We left everything as is."

"Good," Ella replied, barely acknowledging him. Her mind raced with questions. Who was this woman? What had brought her here, to Kennicott? And most importantly, who'd taken her life?

As the crowd reluctantly dispersed, she knelt down beside the body and began to examine it more closely. The investigation had only just begun, and she couldn't shake the feeling that there was far more to this case than met the eye.

The last of night tried to hold back the rising sunlight; the velvet darkness of midnight draped over the ghost town, broken only by the pinpricks of starlight that flickered coldly in the sky. Ella shivered as she continued her examination of the body, feeling the chill of the night air seep into her bones. The victim's clothing struck her as odd; a simple sundress was hardly appropriate attire for an Alaskan night, even during the summer months. And the school jacket... It looked to be stained with blood.

"Detective, take a look at this," one of the officers called out, holding up a plastic bag containing the victim's personal effects. Ella approached, her gaze immediately drawn to a deck of cards and poker chips nestled among the items. As she pulled them from the bag, she noticed something peculiar—a small smiley face drawn with a sharpie on one of the cards.

"What is this?" Ella asked, turning to the officer.

"Can't say, ma'am," he replied, shrugging. "It was like that when we found it."

Ella frowned, mulling over the possible significance of the smiley face. Was it a message left by the killer? Or simply an innocent doodle?

"Bag and tag everything," she instructed.

Brenner came alongside, watchful but quiet. "Poker chips?" he said, his eyes moving to the run-down saloon across the street. "Like something out of a bad Western," he muttered, eyeing the place with deep suspicion.

Ella just nodded absentmindedly.

Unable to shake the unsettling feeling that something was amiss, Ella decided to explore the surrounding area. The ghost town seemed to loom in the darkness, with its old, dusty, and abandoned buildings casting eerie shadows on the ground. Her boots crunched against the gravel and snow as she ventured further, her flashlight illuminating the forgotten relics of Kennicott's past.

Brenner followed along behind her.

"Maybe I can find some answers here," she muttered under her breath, her curiosity piqued by the decaying structures around her. She approached the dilapidated wooden building, its faded sign barely legible, revealing it as the saloon.

As Ella stepped inside, the musty smell of decay assaulted her nostrils, causing her to wrinkle her nose. A layer of dust coated everything, from the broken shelves to the shattered glass on the floor. She ran her fingers along the countertop, leaving trails through the grime that had accumulated over the years.

"Hasn't been touched in ages," she mused aloud, wiping her hands on her jeans. The wind outside picked up, causing the building to creak and groan, sending shivers down her spine. She pulled her jacket tighter around her, feeling the chill seep into her bones.

"Wait... what's that?" Ella murmured, pausing as her flashlight caught something unusual in the window. Squinting, she moved closer, realizing it was a pattern etched into the dust.

Brenner paused also, his brow furrowed. "Looks like someone's been here..." he muttered.

He approached the window.

The markings seemed in the shape of an arrow. And the arrow directed them towards a set of stairs.

The two of them shared a look, shrugged, and without a word both moved towards the stairs.

Ella felt a knot form in her stomach as she descended the narrow, creaky stairs. The smell of damp earth and mold was thick in the air, causing her to cough. "This must be the place," she muttered, shining her flashlight around the dimly lit basement.

"Damn," Brenner gasped, noticing the broken window latch on the far wall, and the jagged shards of glass that still clung to the frame.

"Someone was trying to escape," she whispered, her voice trembling slightly as she examined the scene. Broken bottles littered the floor, their contents long since evaporated, leaving behind only the ghostly scent of stale alcohol. A pool table stood in the corner, its once-green felt now blackened with age and grime.

Her eyes scanned the room, taking in every detail, from the cobwebs that draped every surface to the rotting wooden bar that seemed to sag under the weight of years of neglect.

She carefully stepped over the shattered glass, approaching the bar, where she found a rusted knife, its blade stained with dried blood.

"Definitely the murder weapon," she murmured, her hands shaking as she picked it up using the outside of an evidence bag. As she turned it over in her hands, she caught sight of something wedged between the floorboards. Crouching down, she pried it loose—a crumpled piece of paper that held a hastily scribbled message.

"Meet me at midnight," it read, and a chill ran down Ella's spine. "This... this can't be a coincidence," she mused, feeling the crushing weight bearing down on her. "But who...?" she trailed off, her mind racing with questions and possibilities. She tossed the note onto the bar. She knew that whatever had happened in this basement was the key to solving the murder case, but the answers still seemed just out of reach.

Ella's heart pounded in her ears as she moved deeper into the basement, the dim light from her flashlight casting eerie shadows on the walls. The air was thick with the scent of dried beer, suggesting more contemporary visitors had been in this basement.

Ella muttered, bending down to examine the dried, dark stains on the floorboards near a table. She gingerly touched one of them, her fingers coming away slightly sticky. Bloodstains. The sight made her stomach churn.

"Gotcha!" she exclaimed, spotting a series of faint smudges near the edge of the table. Ella squinted, tracing the ridged pattern with her fingertip. Fingerprints. Someone had clearly leaned against the table, perhaps during a struggle. The realization sent a shiver down her spine.

"Prints?" Brenner said.

"Looks like." She turned to see where he was standing against the far wall, peering up at a dart board.

"What?" she said.

"Bad shot," he replied.

She frowned and realized he was pointing at a dart a good foot *under* the dart board.

She stared at it, but then shook her head. "Let's get the techies to take the print."

Brenner nodded. "Could be hers."

"Could be the killer's."

"Fair enough."

Ella was about to say more, but she paused.

The faintest sound caught her attention, barely audible above the howling wind outside. A creak, a rustle, something stirring in the darkness just beyond her field of vision.

"Who's there?" Ella called out, her voice cracking with fear and defiance. She gripped the flashlight tightly, her knuckles turning white as she prepared herself for whatever—or whoever—might be lurking in the shadows.

There was no response but an unsettling silence, and the creeping dread that perhaps they weren't alone in this ghost town after all.

Chapter 6

The moon hung low in the sky, casting eerie shadows upon the desolate road where Ghost sat in his truck. He was a man on a mission—a mission that consumed every waking moment of his life. His obsidian eyes scanned the pages of the yearbook before him, flicking back and forth as if searching for something that shouldn't be there. With a face like stone, he whispered to himself, "No, that's not right... not right... NO !"

His truck, an old, rusted thing, creaked softly as it idled along the deserted road. Flurries of snow danced around it, propelled by a chilling wind that pierced through the darkness. Ghost's hand shook slightly as he turned the page of the yearbook but not from the cold. It was a tremor born of obsession.

"Damn," he muttered under his breath, frustration evident in his voice. Years of doing this had honed his senses, making him quick to spot any resemblances between the young faces staring up at him from the glossy pages. But tonight, they all seemed so... unique.

"Can't let 'em get away with it," he thought as he flipped through another page. "They're out there, hiding in plain sight. I know it."

He paused, squinting at two photographs near the bottom of the page. Ghost's lips twisted into a cruel smile as he tapped the photos with one dirty fingernail, marking them.

"Gotcha," he whispered triumphantly, the word barely audible even to his own ears. His breathing quickened as he stared at the two faces, his mind racing with thoughts on how to carry out his self-appointed duty.

"Two lives," he reasoned with himself, "Luck of the draw..." He tucked his tongue inside his cheek, and with a shaking hand, pulled a small, copper die from his pocket.

He fiddled with the thing, staring at the six-sided cube.

Ghost's fingers twitched with anticipation as his mind whirled with the possibilities. His breathing was ragged as he tossed the dice up into the air, watching as it spun around and around before finally landing on the floor of his truck with a loud clink.

With bated breath, he leaned over to see which side it had landed on.

"Come on, come on," he muttered under his breath, and then he saw it.

The number three.

A wicked smile spread across his face as he reached for the steering wheel. The truck's engine growled, kicking up snow and gravel as it lurched forward down the lonely road.

Ghost had made his decision, and he knew exactly where he was heading.

The wind howled outside the truck, its mournful wail echoing the darkness within Ghost's soul. He sat there in the cold, hunched over the yearbook, plotting and scheming until the first rays of sunlight began to creep over the horizon.

He kept glancing through the windshield, doing his best to keep his eyes on the road but struggling to do so.

Ghost's hands shook with excitement as he fumbled to uncap the red and blue sharpies. He felt his heart thud against his ribs, a rhythmic reminder that he was doing what needed to be done. With meticulous precision, he circled the girls' faces in the yearbook—one red, one blue—marking them as two sides of an equation that could only have one solution.

"Your time is up," he whispered, his breath fogging up the truck window, the chill air seeping in through the cracks. "It's time for balance."

A sudden thump from the back of the truck interrupted Ghost's thoughts, followed by the sound of muffled cries. His eyes darted towards the rearview mirror, where a faint silhouette struggled against her bindings. A thrill coursed through him at the sight, but he quickly suppressed it, knowing there was still work to be done.

"Quiet now," he called out, his voice cold and detached. "You'll understand soon enough. I promise."

The girl's muffled pleas continued, punctuated by the occasional rustle of ropes rubbing against each other. To Ghost, they were like notes in a symphony, a testament to the righteousness of his actions. But still, he couldn't help but feel a pang of regret for what he was about to do.

"Is this really necessary?" he muttered to himself, his fingers drumming against the steering wheel. "She's so young, so full of life... Can't I just let her go?"

But the answer, as always, was no. The universe demanded balance, and Ghost was its instrument. As much as it pained him, he knew he had to follow through with his mission—for the sake of the world and everyone in it.

With a sigh, he turned his attention back to the yearbook, still driving, but indifferent. He'd driven so long, it was like second nature. Time was running out, and he still had so much left to do. As he flipped through the pages, he couldn't help but wonder how many other one-in-a-millions were waiting to be discovered, their existence a cruel mockery of the unique individuals they mirrored.

"Two lives," he reminded himself, his voice barely audible over the girl's sobs. "But only one can continue."

The girl muffled a sob through her gag, tears pooling in the corners of her eyes. Her heart pounded against her chest with every inhale, her hands straining against the tight ropes that bound her wrists.

"STOP CRYING!" Ghost roared, his voice cracking in desperation. "I'm helping you! Don't you understand? Once you're gone, you'll be free. Truly unique."

As he spoke, his fingers traced the edge of the page, searching for more pairs to mark. His voice grew softer, almost tender. "You're special, and you deserve to live without someone else diluting your existence."

Her breath hitched, and she tried to pull herself together. A small whimper escaped from behind the gag, betraying her continued fear.

She shifted, trying to gain some leverage, but the ropes only dug deeper into her skin.

"Please," she attempted to say, her words barely audible through the cloth. "Let me go. My dad's very powerful! He's the governor! He'll pay you!"

Ghost sighed, torn between his sympathy for the girl and his unwavering determination to restore balance. "You don't understand now, but you will," he whispered, his voice barely audible over the hum of the engine. "I promise."

With that, he turned his gaze back to the yearbook, the girl's terrified eyes boring into the back of his head. His hands trembled as he flipped the pages, searching for the next pair to judge. Every stroke of the Sharpie felt heavier than the last, but he knew he couldn't stop.

"Only one can continue," he repeated, like a mantra to keep himself focused. "Only one."

Chapter 7

Ella's pulse raced as she strained to make sense of the sound in the basement. A low, muffled rustle seemed to grow louder with each passing second, and her mind conjured up a thousand sinister possibilities. The air felt heavy and oppressive, like a weight pressing down on her chest.

She remembered once, standing on the side of a cliff before jumping off with only thin material strapped to her back. She tried to relax, breathing slowly, inhaling, exhaling. She could feel herself calming.

As if in response to her ministrations, the basement door creaked open slightly. She tensed, ready for anything; the tension in the room was palpable. It was then that she spotted it—a flash of white fur darting out from the darkness. Relief flooded her veins as she recognized the intruder: a fox.

"Damn," she muttered under her breath. "It's just a fox."

"Really?" Brenner replied, smirking in the shadows at her side. "Guess we're chasing foxes now."

"Better than chasing shadows," Ella shot back, her grip on her weapon relaxing ever so slightly.

With a nod, Brenner conceded, but his eyes remained watchful. The fox's sudden appearance left an uneasy feeling.

The fox bolted from a small side room, its beady eyes locking onto Ella for a split second before continuing its frantic escape. Ella instinctively tensed again.

"Wait," she murmured, her gaze shifting between the side room and the path the fox had taken. "Why would a fox be in there?"

"Good question," Brenner agreed, his own curiosity piqued.

Brenner nodded, signaling for Ella to stay behind him as they cautiously approached the side room. His thumb hovered over the safety of his gun, ready to flick it off if danger appeared. Ella's heartbeat quickened, her senses sharpening in response to the heightened tension. The air felt heavy and oppressive, making each breath a conscious effort.

As they entered the room, the smell of dampness and decay assaulted their nostrils. A single beam of light from the cracked door illuminated the space, casting eerie shadows across the wooden floor. In the far corner, an unzipped sleeping bag lay rumpled and abandoned. Ella's stomach tightened at the sight.

"Look at this mess," Brenner muttered, his eyes scanning the scattered belongings. Among them were old clothes, torn and stained with what could be blood or dirt—or both. He kicked aside a ratty pair of sneakers, revealing a crumpled plastic bag.

"Could be evidence," Ella said, her voice hushed. She crouched down, examining the bag without touching it. "We'll need to call the forensics team."

Brenner glanced around the room once more, taking in every detail. "Whoever was staying here wasn't living a comfortable life, that's for sure."

"Or a safe one," Ella added, her thoughts trailing off to the possible horrors that had befallen the room's occupant.

Did this stuff belong to the murder victim currently being fished from the copper mineshaft?

As she thought this, Ella paused, frowning. She noticed something jutting out beneath the sleeping bag. A worn-out leather wallet, partially hidden beneath a pile of fabric.

"Found something?" Brenner asked, noticing her sudden attention.

"Maybe," Ella replied, crouching down to examine the wallet without touching it. She used a pen to carefully flip it open, revealing an ID card nestled in one of its pockets. "It's an ID."

Brenner stooped next to her, his shoulder brushing hers. He held his phone lengthwise, taking a clear picture of the ID.

"Whose is it?" Ella inquired, leaning closer to get a better look. The dim lighting in the basement cast eerie shadows across the room, making it difficult to discern the face on the card.

"Let's find out," Brenner said. He tapped away at the screen, his brow furrowed in concentration as he accessed the DMV database. Ella hovered over his shoulder, watching intently.

"Here we go," Brenner announced, his surprise evident as the victim's information appeared on the screen. "This is our murder victim."

"Are you sure?" Ella asked, her heart racing despite having anticipated the possibility. "How can you tell?"

"Look at the address," Brenner murmured, pointing at the screen.

Brenner's fingers flew over the screen, searching for more information about their victim. Both of them knew that every detail could make or break the investigation, and there was no time to waste.

The faint glow of Brenner's phone screen cast eerie shadows across his face as he stared at the new information, his brows furrowed in concentration. Ella could see his Adam's apple bob nervously as he swallowed hard, his eyes never leaving the small screen. She felt a sudden rush of apprehension grip her chest, something about Brenner's reaction sending a shiver down her spine.

"Hey," she whispered, her voice barely audible over the low hum of the basement's fluorescent lighting. "What is it? What's wrong?"

Brenner hesitated for a moment, then he tilted the screen toward her, revealing the DMV photo and information attached to the victim's name.

Ella's breath caught in her throat as she studied the image before her. The woman's eyes seemed to bore into her soul, pleading for help even though it was far too late. She noted the address listed under the victim's name, her heart pounding with the undeniable feeling that this case was much more complex than they had initially thought.

"What the hell," she muttered.

Ella couldn't tear her gaze away from the image on Brenner's phone, her heart pounding in her chest as she tried to process what she was seeing. The uncanny resemblance between the murder victim and the kidnapping victim, the governor's daughter, who'd been taken 700 miles from this spot, was impossible to ignore—it was as if they were staring at the same person.

"Could they be... sisters?" Ella ventured hesitantly, her voice barely audible over the sound of their labored breathing.

"Or twins," Brenner added, rubbing his chin thoughtfully.

"I mean..." Ella half turned as if to glance back up the stairs. "It... it's not *her* is it?"

"Who?"

"The governor's daughter."

"You think he kidnapped her in Nome, then flew seven hundred miles to this ghost town, without being seen?"

Ella just frowned, shaking her head. "I... I know it doesn't make much sense. But..." She trailed off. As she stared at the second picture Brenner brought up, she realized her mistake.

No... the girls looked very similar, but they were not the same person.

Lila Hunt, the governor's daughter, was a bit taller, and she had a beauty mark under one eye. Her eyes were a different color, and the slope of her nose was sharper.

But other than that... Christine Nelson, the murder victim, looked so similar it was uncanny.

"So... our killer has a type," Brenner said softly. "But why would someone go through the trouble of abducting one girl and killing her doppelgänger?"

"Maybe to throw us off their trail?" Ella suggested, her mind racing with possibilities. She could feel the adrenaline coursing through her veins, igniting a fierce determination to uncover the truth, no matter how twisted or dangerous it might be. "Maybe... maybe he thought we'd think this girl was Lila?"

"He'd know we'd check DNA. Check dental."

Ella sighed, shaking her head.

"Besides," he waved his phone, indicating the two pictures side by side. "They're close, but not an exact match."

"So then some twisted motive."

"Either way, we need to find out everything we can about this girl." Brenner's eyes met hers in steely resolve. "And fast."

They exchanged silent nods, both understanding the gravity of the situation. The stakes had been raised, and the urgency to solve the case had intensified. Not just a kidnapping... but a murderer. Two so far... But was this killer a serial offender?

As they stood there, enveloped by the oppressive silence that seemed to amplify every breath they took, Ella felt an overwhelming sense of dread gnawing at the pit of her stomach.

"Alright," Brenner said suddenly, breaking the heavy silence. "Let's get back upstairs. I'll call the forensics to bag and tag."

Ella agreed, her thoughts already racing ahead to the myriad questions they needed answers to. Who was this girl? What was her connection to the kidnapping victim? And, most importantly, could they still save the governor's daughter before it was too late?

Chapter 8

The wind howled through the decaying structures of Kennicott Ghost Town, carrying with it a biting chill that gnawed at Ella's exposed skin. She pulled her scarf tighter around her neck and peered down at the body sprawled across the snow-covered ground, her eyes narrowing as she tried to make sense of the scene before her.

The coroner hadn't arrived yet. Portions of Alaska weren't connected by main roads, and so they were helicoptering in the nearest coroner. A man Ella didn't know.

They'd returned to the body of Ms. Nelson, and Ella was frowning as she knelt beside the corpse, careful not to disturb the surrounding snow. A young woman, no older than twenty. Her face was pale, almost blending in with the icy backdrop, but there was a look of terror forever etched on her features. The cause of death wasn't immediately apparent, but one thing was clear, this girl had suffered.

"Take a closer look at her face," Brenner said, stepping closer. "I can see the differences now. She's a different girl."

"Yeah... yeah, I know." Ella stared down at the figure. Over the girl's simple, pale dress, she wore the school jacket. A school hundreds of miles away... So how had it ended up here?

"What about the jacket she's wearing," Brenner continued, as if reading her mind, pointing to the victim. "That might be our ticket to finding out who this girl is."

Ella frowned, her gaze fixated on the bright, blood-red fabric. It stood out against the pristine whiteness of the snow like a beacon, drawing unwanted attention to its owner. Maybe that's what the killer had wanted—a statement, a show of power.

"Right," she agreed, her voice steady despite the turmoil raging inside her. "We'll get forensics on it as soon as we can."

As they continued examining the scene, Ella couldn't shake the feeling that the murderer was watching them, hidden somewhere among the skeletal remains of the ghost town. The weight of his gaze pressed down on her, smothering her, making it difficult to breathe.

But she refused to let fear stop her. This monster had taken a life. And now it was up to them to stop him.

She took pictures of the jacket and sent the images back to Nome. She texted Chief Baker, *Found in Kennicott. How?*

She breathed slowly, rising to her feet now, and turning to look at the rest of the ghost town.

"Let's check out the rest of this place," she murmured.

Brenner nodded in agreement.

Ella's breath fogged up in the frigid air as she and Brenner worked their way through the ghost town, moving from one dilapidated building to another. The sound of their footsteps crunching in the snow was the only noise that broke the eerie silence, save the occasional sound of a car door slamming as the forensic units scurried about the crime scene.

"Over here," Brenner called out, his voice echoing off the weathered walls. Ella joined him by a crumbling stone structure, its windows long shattered and its roof caving in under the weight of the snow. The wind whispered through the gaps, creating an unearthly moan that sent shivers down her spine.

"Look at this," Brenner said, pointing to the ground. "Footprints, fresh ones too."

As the sun painted the sky with hues of pink and gold, the atmosphere around them shifted. The frozen landscape seemed to come alive, transforming from a lifeless void into a world filled with stark beauty. The mountains loomed above them, their jagged peaks casting long shadows over the winding valleys below.

"Where do you think this will take us?" Brenner asked, scanning the horizon as they followed the footprints in the snow. His keen eyes were always searching, always seeking for something hidden beneath the surface.

"Only one way to find out," Ella replied, straining her own eyes against the brightening light.

They continued onward, carefully stepping over rocks and navigating the treacherous terrain as they ascended. Brenner pointed out specific areas of interest along the way: a twisted tree that seemed out of place in the barren landscape, an abandoned mine shaft half-buried beneath an avalanche of snow.

"Any one of these spots could be significant," Brenner mused. "But be careful. The mountain can be as dangerous as any killer."

"Somewhat rich coming from the guy with bandages under his sleeves."

He shrugged back at her. "We gonna talk about that now?"

She winced. It hadn't been her intention to bring up the subject.

Someone had taken a shot at her. And to get to her, they'd used Brenner. They'd nearly burned him alive, and then had lain in wait to snipe them.

They were lucky to still be alive.

She frowned, shaking her head and letting out a long breath. It was the conversation she'd dreaded.

"Maybe..." she said, her voice hoarse. How could she say it? How could she tell him it was fine... he could break up with her. She knew he'd have to, wouldn't he? Who in their right mind would stay with a marked woman?

Someone out there, someone powerful wanted her dead. She was a liability.

No... No, perhaps it was best she save him the trouble. If she broke up with him, it would keep him safe, wouldn't it?

She opened her mouth again to speak.

But Brenner cut her off. "We should move in together," he said quickly.

She blinked, mouth unhinged.

"Wh-what?"

"Move in together," he repeated, not quite meeting her gaze. He winced. "Just... if you want. It would allow us to keep an eye on each other. You know. Backup."

"Backup, sure..." She trailed off, staring at him.

His handsome features were flushed, his cheeks red. His blue eyes kept darting along the mountain path they strolled down, trying to look anywhere but in her direction.

She found his words melted something in her, like the sun on ice.

He didn't want to break up... he wanted to get closer.

She almost found her lips twisting into a smile, despite the setting, despite where they were.

She shook her head, "I mean... Really?"

"Yeah. Really."

Ella felt a warmth spread through her chest, chasing away the frigid cold that had been clawing at her.

"Okay," she said, smiling for real this time. "Let's... Let's think about it." She hesitated. "Will... will you be safe?"

"What?"

It was as if the question hadn't even occurred to him. Then he blinked. His eyes widened. "You're worried about me?"

"Brenner, I almost saw you burned alive yesterday."

"Pssh. It was nothing."

"It didn't look like nothing." She frowned.

"So is that a yes?" he asked. "We've already established I don't have my own place. And I don't exactly wanna go back and live in my dad's trailer."

Ella smiled, shaking her head. But the smile didn't last long. She knew Brenner's history with his father. It wasn't a laughing matter.

"I... I'd really like that," she said quietly. "But I'm still in a motel."

He threw back his head and laughed. A crystal, clear sound. "My place is burnt, and your place is a motel. Look at the two of us!"

She smiled at him.

Brenner grinned back, looking both relieved and excited. For a moment, they walked in silence, just enjoying the beauty of the landscape around them. But the peace was fleeting and soon they were back to the serious matter at hand.

They followed the footprints up a steep incline, the snow crunching beneath their boots as they went. The path was winding and treacherous, but they climbed it with ease. Brenner moved ahead of her, his athletic form bounding over the rocky terrain.

Ella followed behind, her gaze scanning the snowy expanse for any sign of their quarry. The footprints were gone now. The mountains towered above them, their peaks lost in the clouds, and she felt a sense of awe and insignificance that threatened to overwhelm her.

They were up against not only a ruthless murderer but also the unforgiving elements themselves. It was a deadly combination, and if they weren't careful, they might become the next victims.

The mountains had once been a sanctuary for her, a place where she could escape from the stresses of her job and the chaos of the world below. Now, it felt as if those same peaks were closing in on her, trapping her in a deadly game of cat and mouse with a killer who was always one step ahead. She just hoped that this time they would be able to outsmart their prey before it was too late.

As they ventured further into the heart of the mountain, a series of dark openings drew Ella's attention. "Brenner, look!" she exclaimed, her breath visible in the crisp morning air.

"Good eye," Brenner said as they approached the entrance to what appeared to be a network of tunnels. The thick wooden beams supporting the entrance bore the scars of time and the elements, their once-sturdy forms now twisted and warped.

"Looks like an old mining system," Ella remarked, her voice echoing off the damp walls. "Copper mine, right?" She shivered as they stepped inside, the temperature dropping significantly within the confines of the tunnel. A pungent odor of mold and decay filled the air, and the ground beneath their feet squelched with each step.

"Stay close and watch your footing," Brenner warned, his flashlight cutting through the darkness, revealing the uneven floor strewn with rubble and debris.

As they moved deeper into the labyrinth, Ella couldn't shake the feeling that they were being watched. Each whisper of wind carried the sound of distant echoes, and the shadows seemed to dance along the walls, fueled by her unease.

"Whoever killed her could have used these tunnels to stay hidden, off the beaten path," Ella whispered, the weight of the realization settling heavily on her chest.

"I don't see signs of habitation," Brenner replied, his eyes scanning every corner for potential threats.

"Wait!" Ella called out suddenly as something caught her eye. A shift in the ground under his foot. Brenner stopped in his tracks, turning back toward her.

She tried to snag his arm, to pull him back.

But too late.

Brenner took a step toward the alcove but, without warning, the earth beneath him gave way, and he disappeared into a gaping hole with a yelp of surprise.

Chapter 9

The Ghost stood in the shadows, hidden among the trees at the truck stop. His eyes were fixed on the screen of his phone, watching live security footage from a camera he had set up earlier. He was tall and lean, with dark hair that fell over his forehead, partially covering his cold, calculating eyes. He clenched his jaw in frustration as he saw the police combing through the crime scene where he left his last victim. They had found her too quickly; just a stroke of bad luck.

"Damn them," he muttered under his breath, shifting his weight from one foot to the other. He was far from a gambler, but he couldn't help but admire the chaos of it all.

From the back of his truck came muffled screams, high-pitched yet barely audible. The sound was gut-wrenching, desperate, and raw. It pierced through the air like a knife, intensifying with each passing second before fading away into a whimper. The girl's cries for help only served to fuel the Ghost's excitement. But he needed to find a way to outsmart the police, to throw them off his trail so he could continue his game.

"Let's make this interesting," the Ghost whispered to himself, smirking. He approached the back of the truck, the girl's screams growing louder as he neared. "You want to live? Then you better hope Lady Luck is on your side."

He swung open the truck door and hopped inside, plopping down, butterfly-legged on the cold metal. The girl within withdrew, whimpering as she did, her back pressed against the cold metal. She stared at him, eyes wide.

"Sit," he snapped.

She shrunk back into the shadows, breathing heavily.

He pointed. "Sit," he repeated, more forcefully.

She complied, slowly, a faint breath escaping her lips

He forced the girl to sit down within striking distance, a deck of cards in hand. Her eyes were wide with terror, tears streaming down her face as she struggled against the ropes that bound her wrists.

"Have you ever played blackjack?" he said, conversationally.

She just blinked.

"No?" He smiled. "Allow me to explain the rules. You see, there are cards in this deck that will help you and cards that won't. Each round I'll deal us both two cards, and we'll try to get as close to twenty-one as possible without going over. If you win, I'll let you go."

He paused and leaned in, his voice low. "But if I win, well, let's just say it won't be pleasant for you."

The girl shuddered, her eyes darting around the truck as if searching for an escape. But the Ghost had thought of everything; the doors were locked, the windows barred.

"Let's begin," he said, shuffling the deck.

His first two cards were a seven and a queen, totaling seventeen. The girl's were a six and a three, totaling nine. She looked up at him, hope flickering in her eyes.

"You say hit," he said, looking at her.

She opened her mouth, closed it again. Her eyes moved to his closed fist.

"Say hit," he advised once more.

"I... I... *please.* My dad is—"

"No one cares about your daddy, girl!" he screamed in her face. "Now say *hit*!"

"Hit," she whispered.

He laid down another card for her, enjoying the way she flinched. It was a four, bringing her total to thirteen. She was dangerously close to going over twenty-one.

And then it was his turn again. He took another card, hoping for an ace.

"Shit," he said, his eyes narrowed.

The girl's eyes widened as he revealed his hand. "Does... do I win?" she said, her voice tinged with hope. "Please," she begged. "Just let me go."

But he only chuckled. He tossed his cards on the ground between them. Chance and probability. That's all it was. When patterns repeated, the end came.

He sighed, lifting his device once more, ignoring the cards now.

The Ghost's eyes remained glued to his phone, watching the live security footage of police officers swarming around the dilapidated buildings in the old, abandoned ghost town. He had left what he considered to be a masterpiece there—the lifeless body of his last victim.

"Damn them for finding her so soon," he muttered under his breath as he watched the officers scour the area, searching for any clues that might lead them to him. But the Ghost was always careful, leaving nothing behind that could be traced back to him. In his mind, it was all part of the game—the ever-present tension between predator and prey, each side trying to play a game of chance. And yet, as the police spread out, the Ghost couldn't help but feel a pang of unease.

"Time to change the rules," he whispered to himself, casting one last glance at the screen before turning his attention to the bound girl.

He stood to his feet suddenly, in the large truck enclosure, and she gasped sharply as if she'd been slapped.

He towered over her, observing her as if she were nothing more than a pawn in his twisted game. The Ghost wondered what it would take for her luck to run out.

"Please," the girl whispered again, her voice barely audible through her sobs. "Just let me go."

"Your pleas are pointless," the Ghost sneered. "You should have thought of that before."

As he stood there, contemplating his next move, The Ghost couldn't help but be reminded of the gamble he himself was taking—the constant threat of being caught, the need to outsmart the police at every turn. It was a high-stakes game, each side vying for control, and it thrilled him to no end.

"Perhaps I will give you another chance," the Ghost mused, his eyes gleaming with dark amusement. "But only because I enjoy the game."

"I... I won!" she said.

He ignored her.

"I won!" she said, louder.

"Only once," he replied, his voice harsh. "There were *two* of you, don't you see?"

The girl looked up at him, desperation etched across her face. She knew she had no choice but to play along, to cling to whatever slim chance of survival the Ghost might offer her.

"Now thank me."

"W-what?"

"Thank me! I spared you, I took her. So express some damn gratitude!" he yelled.

"Thank you," she choked out, her voice trembling.

He nodded, staring at his phone, watching. And then he stiffened.

Two of the figures were moving off towards the mountain pass.

No... no... no...

They'd find it.

They'd find *it.*

No!

He jumped out of the back of the truck, slamming the doors once more and muffling the screams.

He sprinted around the front of the truck, racing towards the cabin.

He had to hurry.

He had to return to the ghost town before they found it.

Chapter 10

Ella stood frozen, her heart pounding in her chest as she watched Brenner disappear into the darkness below. She rushed to the edge of the hole, shining her flashlight down into the abyss, hoping to see some sign of him.

It was deep, and she spotted movement in the dark. But the way the floor angled out, the movement was just out of sight.

It looked as if he'd hit a muddy ledge and then rolled down a slant in the floor.

Was that him moving?

"I'm fine!" he called out, his voice sounding strained and distant.

"Brenner!" she hollered, her voice echoing through the system. But there was no response, only the sound of dripping water and her own ragged breathing.

Taking a deep breath, Ella reminded herself of her training and forced herself to focus. She had to find Brenner and get them both out of here.

"Fine! It... it looks like there's a path. See it?"

She frowned. She couldn't see *him*, much less a path.

Gripping her flashlight tightly, she made her way down the slippery slope, her shoes sinking into the mud with each step. The tunnel curved sharply to the right, and she followed it, calling out Brenner's name every few steps, hoping to hear a response.

As she turned another corner, her flashlight beam fell on a large chamber. In the center of the room was a pool of water, shimmering in the light. And standing in front of it was Brenner, his back to her.

"Are you okay?" she said urgently, hastening forward.

Mud caked his clothing. He looked as if he'd been crawling through it for hours. But he was alive, and that was all that mattered.

Brenner turned to face her, and in the dim light, she could see the relief etched in his face. "Yeah," he said, his voice hoarse. "I think I just twisted my ankle. But I can make it out of here."

Ella moved closer, studying his face for any signs of injury. "Let me take a look."

He nodded, and she knelt down, shining her flashlight on his ankle. It was reddened, and he didn't limp with any more emphasis than he had before. "You need to take it easy," she said, her heart racing. "Can you walk?"

Brenner winced as he tested his weight. "Yeah... yeah I'm fine. Just... Got distracted." He turned.

So did she.

And then she went still.

The two of them were staring at an underground lake. The scent of water lingered on the air. The moisture in the cave was palpable, hanging on the air like fog. Thick, green moss covered the ceiling and walls of the cave, some of it growing so long that it curled like ribbons over their heads.

Small stones and larger boulders jutted from the murk like teeth.

Except it wasn't the underground lake that had snared their attention.

It was the bones.

So many bones, all floating on the water.

Ella's breathing became harsh and ragged as she took in the grisly scene. Human bones, animal bones, bones of all kinds floating lazily on the surface of the water. It was a chilling sight that sent shivers down her spine.

Brenner stepped closer to her, his eyes scanning the water as he tried to make sense of the morbid sight.

A leering skull bobbed past them.

"Bones... bones don't float, do they?" Ella said carefully, staring as a femur floated by.

Brenner just shook his head. He reached out with a foot, probing at the strange graveyard.

The water splashed, rippling out.

"It's only an inch deep," he murmured. "They're not floating, they're drifting."

She stepped forward and realized he was right. The water looked deep due to the moss along the base of the floor, but it was only an inch in depth, constantly rippling out and causing the bones to move. Weathered, old bones.

She shook her head. "We need forensics down here. I count at least six human remains."

"Yeah... There's other things too. Is that a badger skull?"

"I don't know. What the hell is this place?"

The two of them stood side by side, staring into the dark.

Ella raised her flashlight over the lake of bones, and she spotted strange markings along the walls.

"What is this?" she said, leaning in.

Brenner stood at her side, breathing heavily, the two of them staring towards the markings on the stone.

"The number two..." Brenner said simply.

Ella frowned.

Indeed, the number two was drawn in crude, jarring lines. Again... again... and again.

Ella felt a faint shiver up her spine as she stared from the pool of bones to the numbers.

"What does it mean?" she said.

"See how some of the paint over there is faded?"

"Yeah."

"It means our guy has been active for a lot longer than we first thought. The governor's daughter isn't his first rodeo. Ms. Nelson isn't his first victim."

"You can say that again," Ella murmured, staring at the bones and feeling a cold chill crawl up her spine.

She paused, frowning and staring at the numbers on the wall, but her eyes swept the cavern again, and she spotted something.

It stood out against the floor, wedged against a rock. Just a tattered piece. She nearly missed it.

She approached, slowly, and bent double.

Brenner was busy radioing forensics, giving them their coordinates.

Ella was zeroed in on the item in question.

She lifted it.

A small stub of paper, torn off on the side. A couple of numbers were visible. Some lines and a graphic of half a smiling face.

"What is it?" Brenner called, hanging up.

She turned, glancing at him, and raised it. "A corner from a lotto ticket."

Brenner wrinkled his nose.

"The Clyde brothers are big into gambling," she said slowly.

"You think they're involved?"

"Lila was involved with them," she said. "Those kids back at the school were dealing for the Clydes."

"Gambling and whoring is a lot different than..." Brenner spread his hand to indicate the room.

"I know... I know," she murmured. "But I still think it's worth checking out." She pocketed the stub of the lottery ticket, slipping it into an evidence bag inside her jacket.

And then she turned, feeling a slow tremor along her arms.

"Gonna have to count the skulls," Brenner said softly.

"Forensics can do that," she said swiftly. "We can wait for the IDs."

"You really think the Clyde brothers had something to do with it?"

"Maybe not them. Maybe someone they know. Someone in their crew. They hire thugs, criminals."

"Alright. Shit. I'll follow your lead, Porter."

Ella nodded resolutely, moving back up the slippery, muddy floor, away from the pool of bones.

Criminals or not, the Clyde brothers would have to give her *something*. Because if not, Lila Hunt would end up in another pile of bones.

Chapter 11

The wind howled through the narrow streets of Nome, Alaska as snowflakes danced in the air like lost souls searching for a place to rest. The Clyde brothers' dance club stood like a fortress against the storm, its garish neon sign flickering intermittently, casting an eerie glow across the slush-covered pavement. The establishment was a hive of illegal activities—gambling, prostitution, and whispers of even darker deeds took place within its walls. It served as a beacon, drawing in those who sought the thrill of the forbidden, the desperate, and those who had been weathered by the long Alaskan winters.

Ella surveyed the club from the shadows of a nearby alley, Brenner at her side.

"Still think this is a good idea?" Brenner muttered, his breath visible in the frigid air.

"Positive," Ella replied, her voice steely with determination.

"All this based on a lotto ticket?"

"A lotto ticket found in a mass grave," Ella muttered, frowning. But she shook her head. "Lila worked for these guys."

"Coming from the testimony of a couple of drug-dealing kids."

"Yeah, but I believe them."

Brenner nodded. He was still frowning. In fact, he'd been frowning ever since they'd arrived. He clearly didn't like the idea of putting her in harm's way. His offer to move in together was still fresh on her mind.

She knew he'd always been protective of her, but she also knew she couldn't let fear dictate anything.

Brenner scanned the area, taking note of the sparse foot traffic outside the dance club. He knew that every second spent outside increased their chances of being spotted. "We need to move fast," he urged. "I'll provide overwatch. Find whatever it is we're looking for and get out."

Ella nodded, her eyes narrowing as she studied the building's exterior. She could see security cameras positioned at strategic points along the facade, indicating that there would be more resistance inside than the unsuspecting patrons twirling on the dance floor. She would have to be quick and silent.

"Keep your eyes peeled," Ella warned, her voice barely audible as she slipped from the shadows and began to approach the club. "I have a feeling we're about to stir up a hornet's nest."

The dance club dominated the coastline, the churning waves below throwing back the hot, electric light. Positioned at the edge of a rocky outcrop, the building appeared to teeter precariously above the water, as though daring the ocean to claim it. The pounding surf echoed the thump of bass from within, creating an eerie harmony that sent shivers down Ella's spine.

Behind the imposing structure, a series of large lobster boats bobbed in the darkness. Their hulls, slick with saltwater and algae, groaned beneath the weight of their heavy, metal traps. One boat, situated closer to the shore, seemed to sway in time with the music. Its windows were lined with red velvet curtains, a beacon of hedonism amidst the utilitarian backdrop.

Ella knew all too well that one of the boats was used as a floating brothel.

As she approached the dance club, Ella could feel the adrenaline coursing through her veins, urging her into action. But she knew better than to let her emotions drive her. She needed to be strategic, precise, and focused if she was going to gather the intel they needed. They still hadn't received IDs on the corpses found back near the ghost-town.

"Stay sharp," Ella muttered to herself, steeling herself for the task at hand.

Keeping low and moving silently, Ella hugged the side of the building while Brenner watched from a safe distance, binoculars glued to his eyes. Her breath came in measured puffs, each exhale forming a ghostly cloud that drifted around her face. She couldn't afford to make a mistake, not with so much at stake.

"Two guards by the main entrance," Brenner murmured into her earpiece, his voice steady as a rock. "Wait for my signal."

"Copy that," Ella whispered back, pressing her body against the cold, rough wall. The uneven texture of the bricks dug into her skin, but she barely noticed the discomfort; her focus was solely on her objective.

"Go now," Brenner said, and Ella didn't hesitate. She darted across the alleyway, ducking behind a stack of wooden crates piled haphazardly near the club's side door. As she caught her breath, she could hear the muffled laughter and music from inside the club, a world away from the tense silence outside.

"Okay, I'm in position," Ella reported, keeping an eye on the two guards posted at the entrance. She knew she needed to find another way in, but time was running out; they had to act fast.

"Ten meters to your left, there's a vent you can crawl through," Brenner advised, his eyes scanning the area through his binoculars. "It should lead you straight to the main office."

"Got it," Ella replied, spotting the vent and quickly making her way towards it. She crouched down, using a discarded rebar piece from an old construction project to pry the metal grate free. It groaned in protest, but she managed to keep the noise to a minimum. With one last glance at the guards, she slipped inside.

As she crawled through the narrow passage, her heartbeat thundered in her ears, drowning out everything else. But then, just as she was about to turn a corner, she heard voices. They were hushed and tense, the words barely audible.

"Keep your voice down," the other guard snapped, a hint of fear in his tone. "You know what'll happen if the boss hears you talking like that."

"That lil' bitch brought more trouble than good. What was he thinking?"

"Governor's welp in his pocket was what he was thinking," came the quick reply.

"Man... shit. I don't get paid enough for a federal rap."

The voices trailed off, still murmuring dark contemplations.

Ella's blood ran cold at the mention of the governor's daughter. She pressed herself against the vent, willing her breathing to quiet as she strained to hear more.

"Look, just do your job and keep your mouth shut," the second guard continued, his words laced with barely concealed panic. "The Clydes didn't get to where they are by being careless. We'll be fine... as long as nobody screws up."

"Right," the first guard muttered, though, he didn't sound convinced. "I just don't like it, that's all."

Neither do I, Ella thought, her heart pounding even harder now. They were being sufficiently vague, but clearly, even the henchmen knew of Lila Hunt's disappearance and her involvement with their outfit.

Ella inched along the vent, her heart thundering as she considered her options. The guards' nervousness was contagious.

She muttered under her breath, wiping a bead of sweat from her forehead.

She reached the end of a grate, pushing her hand against it. The vent connected to a dark hallway. She took a couple of quick glances but saw nothing to alarm her. Her eyes darted around, searching for a clue as to where the main office might be. That's when she noticed the security cameras.

"Always follow the eyes," Brenner had told her once, and now those words echoed in her mind. If she could trace the cameras back to their source, she'd find the control room—and hopefully, the information she needed.

"Okay, Ella," she whispered, steeling herself. "You've got this."

Creeping along the shadowy edge of the hallway, Ella carefully studied the angles of the security cameras. As she moved, she noted how they were all pointed towards a central location: a nondescript door tucked away in a corner.

"Gotcha," she breathed, her pulse quickening with excitement. It had to be the main office.

She tried the door; with a soft click, the lock disengaged, and she slipped inside.

The office was small and cramped, its walls lined with monitors displaying live feeds from the various security cameras. A single desk occupied the center of the room, its surface cluttered with papers and cold cups of coffee. At the far end, a large computer tower hummed softly, casting an eerie glow across the space.

"Alright, time to dig up some dirt," Ella said to herself, pulling a small USB drive from her pocket. She knew she didn't have much time—the guards could return at any moment, and she still had to make her escape.

As she plugged the drive into the computer, she couldn't help but think of what was at stake. If the Clyde brothers really were connected to the governor's daughter, that was one thing. But if they'd kidnapped her? If they were involved with the murders?

She shivered.

"Come on, come on," she urged the computer as it copied files onto her USB drive. Her breath came in shallow gasps, her eyes darting between the door and the progress bar on the screen.

Her heart raced with anticipation as she waited for the computer to finish its task. She knew she was treading dangerous waters, but she was in too deep now. There was no turning back.

As the files transferred, Ella took in more of the room around her. The dimly lit office had an air of neglect, with dust covering every surface and papers strewn about haphazardly. A large window looked out onto the bridge of one of the lobster boats, illuminated by flickering fluorescent lights on the vessel.

Her brow furrowed at the eerie stillness of the boat. Why was there no activity out there?

The sound of footsteps echoing through the hallway outside the office snapped her back to reality. Heart pounding, she dove behind a small desk just as the door swung open. Two burly men entered the room, reeking of cigarettes and cheap cologne. Ella held her breath, praying they wouldn't find her hiding spot.

"Boss said we gotta," one of the men grumbled, his voice low and gravelly. "With all these cops around, we can't afford any screw-ups."

"Fine," the other replied, his voice dripping with irritation. "Let's get it over with."

Ella watched from behind the desk as the men approached the computer. She knew she couldn't let them find the USB drive, but what could she do?

As the men surveyed the computer, Ella's mind raced for some way to distract them. Her eyes landed on the coffee cups scattered on the desk.

With a deep breath, she steadied herself and slipped her hand up from her hiding spot, grabbing one of the cups and sending it flying across the room with all her might. The cup shattered against the wall, drawing the men's attention.

"What the hell?" one of them growled, his eyes scanning the room for the source of the disturbance.

As they both moved towards the shattered cup, Ella took her chance and darted towards the computer. She quickly removed the USB drive and slipped it back into her pocket.

"Shit, it's just a cup," the other man muttered, his eyes narrowing as he surveyed the room. "Did it fall?"

The man was staring, clearly a bit slower than his boss might've preferred.

Back in her hiding spot, Ella held her breath, praying they wouldn't find her. But as the men advanced towards her hiding spot, she knew she had to act fast. They kept coming closer.

Closer.

One began leaning and was going to peer under the desk. She'd be spotted. So she took a chance.

She grabbed another cup and hurled it towards the man this time.

The cup hit one of the men in the forehead. He yelped, stumbling back.

"What the hell?" he yelled, his finger hovering over his trigger.

Ella's heart was pounding now, and she knew she had only seconds before the men gathered their wits enough to grab her. She quickly scanned the room for an escape route, spotting a window on the far side of the room.

Without hesitation, she lunged towards the window, breaking through the glass with a loud crash. Glass shattered everywhere as she tumbled onto the deck of the lobster boat, the icy ocean spray stinging her face

Loud shouts echoed behind her.

The docks loomed ahead, the lobster boats casting eerie shadows across the water. Ella could hear the faint laughter and music from the club, a stark contrast to the pulsating dread that consumed her.

As she sprinted towards the docks, Ella knew she had to take a moment to catch her breath. She ducked behind a stack of crates, listening for any sounds of pursuit. The cold night air was biting, causing her to shiver.

Peering around the crates, she could see the yellow light of the club nearby. She had to get there, back to Brenner and backup.

She stepped out from behind the crates, just in time to see the two burly men from the office emerge from the same doorway she'd just escaped. They were shouting into their radios, no doubt alerting the rest of the organization that they had an intruder. Ella's adrenaline surged, catapulting her into action. She had to run.

Crouching low, Ella sprinted towards the club, her body poised for any sudden movements. She could hear the men's footsteps pounding against the pavement, getting closer and closer with each passing second.

Fear had faded now. Adrenaline remained. She often found, in the tense moments that her mind would focus in sharply.

And then two more men appeared on the dock in front of her.

She froze.

Two behind, guns drawn.

Two ahead, also armed.

Shit.

She glanced back, and the men were surging towards her. The one she'd hit with the cup was bleeding from his cheek and snarling. He raised his weapon.

Double shit.

Making a split-second decision, Ella dove into the frigid water.

Chapter 12

Her muscles screamed in protest as the icy waves closed over her head, but she forced herself to stay submerged, eyes wide open and trained on the lobster boat serving as a brothel to the East. Its hull gleamed like the enormous eye of a predator in the moonlight.

All sound faded now, swallowed by the water.

The cold ate at her. Hypothermia could set in within seconds. She urged herself silently, legs kicking furiously beneath the surface.

She couldn't hear the shout of pursuers. She felt a flicker of gratitude for zipping her waterproof jacket pocket. The USB would be safe.

But the same couldn't be said for her.

Ella's lungs were on fire, but she couldn't afford to surface just yet. She could see the lobster boat nearby, its shadow looming ominously beneath the water. She swam towards it with all her might, her heart racing as she struggled to stay afloat in the frigid water.

Finally, after what seemed like an eternity, she reached the boat's hull and clung to a metal rung on a Jacob's ladder, gasping for breath. She knew she was in dangerous waters, but she had nowhere else to go.

As she clung to the side of the boat, she heard the sound of footsteps on the dock above. They were getting closer.

With a deep breath, she pulled herself up the ladder, moving swiftly, shedding water in sheets. The chill cold bit at her, like canine teeth gouging into her flesh. But she couldn't slow. Not now. She dragged herself onto the boat's deck and peeked cautiously over the edge. Six men on the wharf now.

Where did they keep coming from?

She ducked out of sight again before they spotted her. Their guns gleamed in the moonlight.

Scanning the deck, she spotted a door leading inside the boat. Without hesitation, she darted towards it and pushed it open. The room inside was dimly lit, with a single lamp casting ghostly shadows across the walls.

Ella's breath caught in her throat as she took in the scene before her.

It was like a waiting room at a doctor's office.

Chairs set along the walls. Figures lounging in the chairs. The room was filled with men, all of them leering at her with lustful eyes. She knew what kind of business was conducted on this boat, and the thought made her skin crawl.

But she had no time to waste. She darted past the men, searching for any sign of an escape route.

One of the men tried to reach out and grab her arm. She shoved him and sent him clattering into a chair.

He toppled to the ground and his friends laughed.

The other clientele in the room were either too drugged out or too horny to react.

Ella bolted past them, out the other side of the waiting area onto the opposite deck. The railing here was cast in shadow.

And there, ahead of her, she spotted a figure.

A lone, lanky figure gesturing hurriedly at her.

She blinked.

Brenner Gunn.

And at his feet, two unconscious men.

Clearly, her overwatch hadn't been idle.

She felt a thrill of relief, and, still trembling horribly, sprinted along the deck. She couldn't feel her fingers now. Everything felt numb.

She bolted down the metal ramp, her feet clanging.

"Shit, what happened?" Brenner hissed, staring at her.

She tried to speak, but her teeth were chattering too hard. She just stumbled against him, and he helped support her.

The two of them broke across the dock, hidden in the shadow of the vessel.

She could hear the sound of other pursuers on the boat, heavy, booted footsteps clanging on metal walkways.

But Brenner and Ella didn't slow.

They moved fast.

Faster still, racing away towards their vehicle.

Her hand clutched at the USB in her pocket.

Bank files, employment statements, security footage. She'd gotten everything she could.

If anything would tie the Clyde brothers to Lila Hunt's disappearance, it would be this.

She could only hope it had been worth it.

And that she didn't lose any toes from frostbite like her cousin Maddie.

Trembling horribly, she slipped into their waiting vehicle and felt relieved to realize Brenner had left it running, the heat blasting.

He snatched a blanket from the emergency kit in the back, throwing it at her with quick, decisive motions.

"Risky, Porter," he said.

"Yeah," she managed to say between chattering teeth. "But I got everything."

"Everything?"

"Well... like twenty gigs of stuff." She paused, shivering again, and holding her trembling fingers to the heated vents.

"Yeah? Shit..." Brenner stared at her but seemed to relax as the bluish tinge to her skin was warmed by the vents. He watched her closely and then said, "Report came in while you were there."

"What?"

"They identified some of the bodies."

She stared at him, still trembling, blanket wrapped over her trembling form, heat blasting. Brenner now put the car in gear and began moving away from the docks.

"From the mineshaft?" she said.

"Yeah."

"What... what did they find?"

He just shook his head as if bewildered. "You're going to have to see it to believe it."

Chapter 13

As the small charter plane traversed across the Alaskan wilderness towards the Kennicott Ghost Town once again, Ella couldn't shake the chill from her bones, despite the warm air blasting from the vents above her.

Below, a dark expanse of treacherous terrain spread out before them.

Ella glanced over at where Brenner was sleeping, his head lolled to one side. Her laptop was on the small seat between them, a buckle thrown over the white keyboard.

Her eyes drooped slowly, and she stifled a yawn. She'd managed to snag a couple hours of sleep in their night-time journey. But the sun was still dormant, and the dark skies held little in the way of reprieve for her troubled mind.

She glanced back at the computer screen between her and her snoring partner.

She picked up the laptop, frowning again as she cycled through the victim reports.

Eight victims had been identified from the mineshaft.

All of them women. All in their twenties.

And all of them...

A match.

Doppelgangers.

Identical... except they weren't twins. Weren't even related. Some of the women had been from the lower forty-eight. Others from Alaska. She began to scroll through the images, one by one, her nerves frayed.

The first two victims had coal-black hair. They had *some* differences, for sure. But the differences were marginal at best. One with an up-turned nose, the other with a slightly straighter nose. But their eyes were the same color. The same heart-shaped faces. The same slender bodies. They could have been sisters, perhaps, but the DNA tests proved otherwise.

Ella focused on the third victim, a woman with blonde hair and wide-set blue eyes. She had a small scar above her right eyebrow, but apart from that, she could have been mistaken for the fourth woman. "Alice Grace," Ella whispered softly, her fingers touching lightly to the keyboard.

The killer was targeting doubles. Doppelgangers. The victim they'd found with the lotto ticket in the ghost town looked identical to Lila Hunt, the governor's daughter.

But Lila's body hadn't been found. She was still alive...

Or so Ella hoped.

So what was the killer up to? The lotto ticket... a game of chance? Of probability?

What were the odds of two victims who looked identical?

It was all a matter of odds...

She frowned, scowling at the computer screen, trying to make sense of all of it.

What did the governor's daughter have to do with it?

Ella couldn't shake the feeling that she was missing something. She leaned back in her seat, running her fingers through her hair as she tried to think. The plane rattled and shook, making her stomach lurch.

Brenner stirred beside her, groaning quietly.

He rubbed a hand over his eyes, his gaze focused on her face. "What time is it?"

"About four in the morning."

He groaned again, sitting up and stretching. "Long night."

"You're telling me."

She gestured towards the computer screen. "I can't figure out what the common link is between all these women."

Brenner leaned in closer, studying the images. "They do look eerily similar."

"That's not the only thing. They all had something else in common."

"What?"

She hesitated for a moment, her fingers hovering over the keyboard. "None of them knew the other."

"What?"

"They didn't know each other. I've been running a social media scan. No common friends. No common locations. These women were all strangers."

"So, what are you thinking?"

"That this killer is targeting women who look alike..." She shrugged. "Not exactly a theory. More an observation."

Brenner leaned back in his seat, running a hand through his hair. "We need more information." He shook his head. "So what about the USB drive?"

"Encrypted," she replied. She frowned, tabbing to another window on the desktop, and checking her email. She shrugged. "Going to take a bit for them to get back to me," she said.

"Shit. Can't they rush anything?"

"This is their version of rushing," Ella said quietly. She frowned. Something about the request for a decryption had caught her attention. Briefly, it had looked as if her email had been forwarded to a higher-up. Was she being watched? Ella had known that someone was keeping tabs on her... but she hadn't known how *closely*. She frowned, her mind moving to Mortimer Graves and her best-kept secret.

She shook her head, returning her attention to the laptop.

And their plane began to dip, suddenly, catching a bout of turbulence.

She hesitated briefly, hand clenching the armrest, and then the plane veered sharply.

Brenner shouted.

And the nose dipped, causing the plane to plummet from the sky.

Chapter 14

The Ghost peered through his binoculars, scanning the decaying buildings of Kennicott Ghost Town in the valley below. His heart raced at the sight of black-suited FBI agents swarming over the rotting wood and crumbling stone like ants on a carcass.

His hands tightened around the binoculars as rage bubbled up inside him. The FBI had no right to invade his sanctuary. They were contaminating it, sullying its purity with their tromping boots.

He slammed the binoculars down on the rocky outcrop, chest heaving. "Get out!" he shouted at the figures in the distance. "Get out now!"

No one heard his furious cries. The FBI continued their work, oblivious to the watcher in the mountains. Oblivious to the danger poised above them, ready to strike like a viper.

The Ghost's hands curled into fists, knuckles turning white under the pressure. He wanted nothing more than to descend into the valley, to confront the intruders and drive them from his territory. But he knew that was foolish. Reckless. He would be captured or killed.

Patience, he told himself. Chance and luck were on his side. The FBI would leave in time. And when they did, he would resume what had been interrupted. The Ghost Town would run red once more.

He picked up the binoculars again, glaring through them at the FBI agents. As his anger mounted, a grim smile twisted his lips.

The wait would make his vengeance all the sweeter.

And then he spotted a figure. A man moving amidst the trees, having distanced himself from the town. The sound of a zipper. The accompanying *ahh* of satisfaction as the agent began to relieve himself.

A Fed. Fifty paces away. None the wiser to the Ghost's presence.

But what to do?

To run? To hide?

To approach?

"Chance, my old friend," the Ghost whispered, pulling a worn silver dollar from his pocket. "You've never let me down before."

The moonlight glinted off the coin as it spun in the air. The Ghost watched intently as the coin landed on heads—the sign for action.

"Fortune favors the bold," he mused, as he crept closer to the unsuspecting agent. His movements were steady and silent, like a predator stalking its prey. In these moments, his anger was eclipsed by a cold, calculating focus.

"Hey, Jim! You find anything?" called another agent from a distance.

"Nothing yet," the isolated agent replied, zipping up his pants, unaware of the Ghost's approach.

"Keep looking, man—might be another one of those mineshafts!" the distant agent shouted back.

As the agent turned around, the Ghost pounced. With one swift motion, he grabbed the man by the mouth, stifling any cries for help. The sharp edge of his trusty switchblade found its mark at the base of the agent's neck, silencing him forever.

"Sorry, Jim," the Ghost whispered into the lifeless ear. "Bad luck."

He carefully dragged the agent's body to a nearby thicket, concealing it beneath a pile of leaves and branches. The Ghost glanced back at the ghost town, his desire to return burning brighter than ever.

With each passing moment, the Ghost grew bolder, embracing the dark power that chance and luck bestowed upon him.

He studied the bloodied corpse, calculating his next move. He couldn't let the FBI discover the body just yet—it would only amplify their efforts to find him. He needed a disguise.

"Sorry, Jim," The Ghost muttered, peeling the dead agent's clothes off his limp form. "I need these more than you do now."

He dressed himself in the blood-stained uniform, buttoning up the shirt and adjusting the belt. It wasn't perfect, but it would do. As he removed his previous attire, he took a moment to examine the coin in his hand. Heads or tails? Fortune had brought him this far; surely, it wouldn't abandon him now.

"Show me the way, Lady Luck," he whispered, flipping the coin into the air.

It caught the waning sunlight as it spun, and when it fell back into his palm, the answer was clear. Heads.

The Ghost narrowed his eyes with determination.

He scrubbed at his collar, flicking warm blood away. The smear of bronze would have to be hidden by the jacket. He zipped it up, high, the bright yellow FBI logo displaying on his sleeve and his back.

As he treaded cautiously toward the ghost town, he spotted a small plane descending towards a makeshift runway. His heart tightened within his chest, a grimace etching itself across his face. More agents, no doubt. But he couldn't turn back now. Not when he was so close.

"Hey, you!" a voice called out from behind him, forcing the Ghost's pulse to race. "Where the hell is Jim?"

"Uh, he's, uh... taking a leak," the Ghost replied, trying to sound casual. He didn't glance back. "Said he'd be right back."

"Damn it," the strange voice muttered. "Well, come on, we've got work to do."

"Right," the Ghost said, his heart pounding as he followed the agent toward the ghost town. "Let's get to it."

As they walked, the Ghost couldn't help but marvel at how luck had once again played in his favor. He knew that he would have to rely on that force to guide him.

The same couldn't be said for the plane above. He stared at it, mumbling under his breath.

And then the plane hit a patch of turbulence and began to dive. He watched, curious as the plane plummeted.

A couple of other agents were looking up, concern etched across their features. But he allowed himself a smile.

Fate seemed to be on his side in more ways than one. The plane whined above him, cutting through the dark sky.

His mind wandered away from something so inconsequential to his thoughts. His eyes moved back to the ghost town.

Of course... he'd made a promise once.

If anyone found his hiding spot...

He'd burn the whole place to the ground. And he'd do it with them all in it.

Chapter 15

The small plane continued to dip, catching another updraft. Ella and Brenner both gripped the edges of their seats, staring towards the cockpit.

"We good, pilot?" Brenner shouted.

A pause then a crackle of static and a voice over the intercom. "Please remain seated. We're engaging in an impromptu landing."

The voice tried to speak calmly, but Ella could detect the fear in it.

The plane continued to dip, veering sharply, and Ella felt her shoulder brush tightly against the window of the plane. There, far below, she spotted the ghost town. Bright beams of light from search parties illuminated portions of the ruined structures.

The sun still hadn't arrived yet.

"Hold on tight!" the voice said over the intercom.

And then the plane made a whining sound against the wind as it moved in for a crash landing.

Ella gritted her teeth but refused to look away—her eyes peered out the window, watching the terrain far below. The landing was rough, sending Ella and Brenner jolting in their seats. The plane shuddered and jolted wildly as the tires hit the landing strip. Ella's knuckles turned white from her grip on the armrest, and Brenner was gritting his teeth to muffle a curse. The plane screeched to a halt, and for a moment, they sat there in silence, waiting.

"Everyone okay back there?" the voice called out over the intercom.

Ella exhaled a breath, relieved. "We're good," she called back.

She looked over at Brenner, his face was pale. "You okay?" she asked him.

Brenner nodded, but his eyes were wide. A second later, they narrowed in irritation, and she watched in real-time as he chose anger over fear.

It took them both a few seconds to trust they could gain their feet.

When they did, Ella glanced out the window. One of the engines was smoking.

"What are the odds," she muttered under her breath.

Brenner gave her a long look, then shook his head. The two of them moved cautiously towards the exit.

It felt strange to disembark from a plane that had nearly crashed into the ground.

Ella shook her head, finding that her emotions were only now catching up with the processing of her mind.

"That was close," she muttered.

Brenner didn't reply.

The captain remained at the front, still gripping the controls and yammering away into a headset, filling someone in on the incident.

As they stepped out onto the landing strip, Ella squinted against the brightest of the searchlights and surveyed the wasteland before them. The ghost town, barren and desolate, was a far cry from the bustling town she'd left behind.

She turned to Brenner, who was checking their surroundings with suspicious eyes. "What the hell are they still searching for?" Brenner demanded, his hand edging towards his gun.

Ella shrugged. "More graves."

They took a few tentative steps forward, the sound of their feet crunching against the rocky terrain bouncing off the walls of the ruined buildings.

They moved towards the mineshaft they'd found, and ahead, lining the road, they spotted teams of police officers huddled together. Some had already set up temporary shelters and were taking cover, shivering in the breeze. Others were moving in and out of the mineshaft entrance, carrying evidence. And in more than one case, plastic buckets full of bones.

"Careful!" a man was saying, shaking his head and jamming his hands into a puffy overcoat. "Don't disturb the evidence! Careful!" he said, shouting as a younger forensics agent nearly tripped on a jutting root.

Ella approached quickly, Brenner at her side.

They'd found eight bodies in the tunnel. All of them reduced to bones.

By the look of the man in the puffy coat, with his wispy hair, he was in charge.

"Excuse me, sir!" she called out, raising a hand.

The man turned to face her, his nose wrinkling. He shifted uncomfortably from foot to foot, and it was evident by his bunching chin and his discomfort standing still that more than a few pounds clad the frame beneath the coat.

"Ah, yes... Agent Porter?" he said.

She blinked, surprised he'd recognized her. She didn't ask to discover what sort of file he'd been reading. Instead, she extended a hand, keeping her expression pleasant.

Brenner gave her a sidelong glance. He'd always been slightly irritated at how easily she was able to put on a mask, hiding her emotions.

They'd nearly been in a plane crash, but she smiled and shook his hand as if they'd just agreed on some business deal.

Then, she said quickly, "We've been looking over the files. Anything you can tell us?"

The man gave a long sigh, massaging the bridge of his nose and adjusting his glasses which seemed to fog with each breath. He rubbed the edge of his sleeve against the glass, clearing it, before replacing them once more.

"Still preliminary," he said, frowning as another bucket of bones was lugged past him. He clicked his tongue angrily, and the two men hauling the bucket adjusted their grips on the handles, slowing their progress and shooting dirty looks in his direction.

"I'm sorry, we didn't catch your name," Brenner cut in.

The man didn't seem to hear. "Careful!" he yelled, waving at the two men with the bucket. "I need those intact!" He looked back, muttering, "Hooligans," under his breath.

He then glanced at Brenner once more. "Sorry, what was that? Oh, my name? Dr. Connor. Forensics. You two found the bones, yeah?"

Brenner nodded.

Ella crossed her arms. She glanced off towards the ghost town in the distance, the old structures of the abandoned mining community standing out like shipwrecks against the darkness as the sun finally began to rise, glinting over the mountains.

Ella stifled a brief yawn. She'd only managed to snag a couple of hours of sleep on the plane. But her adrenaline was racing through her system.

"Walk with me," Dr Connor said, already moving, and clicking his fingers as if he were attempting to call a dog to heel.

Ella and Brenner shared a look but then fell into step.

"So you've found eight bodies?" Ella asked.

"Ten now," he shot back. "Was hard to determine the type of mammal at first."

"So there were other bones in there?" Ella said.

"Mhmm. Mostly species native to Alaska."

"Mostly? Like what?"

"Some smaller animals. Also caribou," Dr. Connor replied. "But there were some bear bones mixed in there as well."

Ella raised an eyebrow. "Bear bones?"

Dr. Connor nodded. "Yes. Quite a few, actually. And not just any bears. Grizzlies."

Brenner interjected. "You're saying whoever put them there is a hunter, right?"

Dr. Connor shrugged. "It's possible. But there's one thing that doesn't quite add up."

"What's that?" Ella asked.

"Well," Dr. Connor said, pausing for a moment to collect his thoughts. "The skulls all had an etching on them. A four-leaf clover, etched as if with a laser into the bone."

Ella and Brenner exchanged a quick glance.

"That's... unusual," Ella said.

"Very," Dr. Connor agreed. "And it's not just that. Some of the bones show signs of being exposed to fire."

Brenner narrowed his eyes. "Fire?"

"Yes," Dr. Connor confirmed. "Small burns but burns nonetheless."

Ella and Brenner looked at each other again.

"We'll need to look into it further," Ella said, her mind already working through the possibilities. "Thank you for the information, Dr. Connor. There weren't any other burial sites discovered, were there?"

"No. We didn't find any."

Ella felt a slow shiver along her back. For a moment, it almost felt as if they were being watched. She glanced back towards the ghost town once more.

Dr. Connor had turned away from them, haranguing another forensic tech who was taking photos of the trail.

Ella turned to Brenner, and keeping her voice low, she murmured, "What do you think?"

"About what?"

"Any of it?"

"How's he getting out here?"

"Excuse me?"

"Roads are sparse. Few runways. How's he getting out here. How's he bringing his victims?"

Ella hesitated, frowning. "Caribou bones. Bear bones."

"You think he's a poacher?"

She nodded once, impressed that he'd reached the same conclusion. The two of them were on the same wavelength again. She studied his handsome features, and there was a troubled look in his eyes. Whenever young women were the victims, Brenner developed a far-off look to his gaze. He'd lost a child...

And had taken to drinking again.

Until she'd returned to Nome.

Now, he didn't smell of alcohol and regret. But the sadness often still lingered in those pretty eyes.

"So if our guy is a poacher, he has his own way of getting around. Would know back roads. Off-terrain vehicles. Boats. Planes. Whatever..."

Brenner nodded in agreement.

"So what's with the four-leaf clover?" she pressed.

The two of them were moving slowly down the trail, their breath gusting over their shoulders in ashy plumes.

Brenner said, "Luck. A four-leaf clover has to do with luck."

"Brings us back to the gambling halls, doesn't it?"

"Maybe... Maybe not. We hear anything about the Clyde brothers' encrypted file yet?"

Ella glanced down at her phone, pulling it up. She paused. Six missed notifications. Two emails.

She felt a prickle along her hand. "It just came in a few minutes ago," she murmured. "They found something."

Chapter 16

Ella and Brenner sat in an orange tent set up at base camp, both of them leaning forward to study the phone placed on the plastic table between them.

The sun had risen now, and it streamed through the fabric, casting vibrant patterns against the cold ground.

Ella shifted her feet on icy gravel, as the tent didn't come with a floor.

"What does it mean?" Brenner said, scowling.

Ella didn't reply at first, her gaze fixated on the screen as the surveillance footage played again. They'd been playing it on loop for the last ten minutes.

"It's her alright," Ella said quietly. She watched as Lila Hunt moved up the side of the brothel boat she'd seen back at the dance club.

She scrutinized the footage as a young woman, her hair tinged with red dye on the tips, paused to speak to someone out of sight, and then continued along the walkway.

And then Ella clicked on the screen, cycling to a *second* footage stream.

This one was from a week prior. It showed a boat arriving at the dock, near the brothel ship. It showed a small group of tourists disembarking. And it showed another young woman, who looked identical to Lila Hunt, exiting and approaching the Clyde brothers' establishment, a beer in hand, and an easy smile plastered across her face.

Ella clicked back and forth between the two images.

"What does it mean?" Brenner repeated.

"That's our murder victim," Ella said, nodding at the second video with the smiling girl. She paused. "So the Clydes are involved," she said.

"Maybe. Doesn't show that."

"But both girls were at their brothel. Both of them came through. Lila dealt for them. Looks like our murder victim just stopped by for a refuel."

"Doesn't mean it's them," Brenner said with a shrug. "Could just be a point of contact."

Ella frowned. "I still think we need to get them alone in a room. Talk to them."

Brenner tensed. "The Clydes aren't going to come quietly."

"I know," she murmured. She shot him a sidelong glance. The last time they'd tangled with a duo, it had nearly ended with Brenner's death.

She didn't like the idea of returning to Nome, anyway. That was where the hitmen awaited them.

But she also refused to live in fear... She had a job to do, and until proven otherwise, she was going to assume Lila Hunt was still alive.

Ella let out a long, shaky breath, replaying the footage once more.

"See if you can spot anything. Anyone who spoke to the two girls."

"It's just some grainy footage," Brenner replied, rubbing the bridge of his nose. "We've been over it."

She nodded but didn't reply right away. She clicked play again.

As the footage looped, Ella's eyes began to focus on the people moving in the background. She watched as a man in a dark hoodie walked past them, his face hidden behind the hood. He looked normal enough, but something about the way he walked, the way he carried himself stood out to her.

She rewound the video and played it again, watching the man closely. This time, she noticed something else—a glint of silver on his hip.

"Hey, Brenner," she said, gesturing for him to come closer. "Look at this guy. Anything stand out to you?"

Brenner leaned over her shoulder, squinting at the screen. "Just some dude in a hoodie," he said.

"But look at his hip," she pointed out. "You see that?"

Brenner's eyes widened as he noticed the silver object hanging off the man's belt. "Is that a gun?" he asked, his voice low.

Ella nodded, a knot forming in her stomach. "I think it might be."

"Doesn't look like one of the Cyldes. Too thin."

"Could be working for them," Ella said.

She watched as the man in the hoodie disappeared past Lila, moving onto the ship.

A lot of men in Nome carried guns. It didn't mean anything.

She played the footage once more and then let out a long sigh. "Might be good to get it from the horse's mouth," she said softly.

Brenner nodded, but he was glancing at his phone. "Huh," he said.

"What?"

"They're not in Nome."

"How's that?"

"Marshal Bud in Juneau is keeping an eye on air traffic. Their plane just showed up."

"In Juneau?"

"Mhmm."

Ella pushed to her feet, closing the laptop lid. "Let's see what they're doing out of town."

***

The Ghost watched as two peculiar figures moved along the snowy ground, heading towards the airstrip.

He stared at the woman with the blonde hair and upturned nose, blinking a few times.

"What are the odds..." he whispered under his breath.

He pulled his phone from his pocket, fur gloves brushing dappled spots of moisture from the screen, and he cycled to the newspaper for his hometown, Nome.

He recognized the woman... Except it wasn't *her*.

Priscilla Porter... This... this was someone else, though.

He looked up again, staring. A federal agent, walking with some gun thug at her side.

He swallowed briefly, feeling a faint shiver. He took a picture of her, surreptitiously, still wearing the FBI uniform he'd stolen from the agent he'd killed.

For now, no one had found the body. No one seemed to miss the agent either.

He smiled to himself, picking up his pace and moving after the two figures heading to the airfield.

As he walked, his mind raced with possibilities. What were they doing in Juneau? Were they closer to uncovering his identity than he thought? The Ghost had always been meticulous, careful not to leave any loose ends behind. But could he have missed something?

He trailed the two figures from a distance, watching as they approached a small plane. They spoke briefly to the pilot before boarding the aircraft.

The Ghost's heart raced as he pulled out his phone and called his boss.

"Sir, we have a problem," he said, his voice tight.

"What is it?" answered a gruff voice through the speaker.

"The Feds are here. But they're leaving—itinerary says Juneau."

There was a moment of silence on the other end of the line.

"What are they doing coming here?"

"I don't know. But they're heading towards the airstrip. They're leaving now."

"Get on your plane and follow them," Clyde said, his voice steely. "We can't have them messing with shit."

The Ghost felt a cold sweat break out on his forehead as he watched the small plane take off.

His boss didn't know the half of it. Didn't know what he was up to. Didn't know... *anything* really.

But he was a useful fool.

He clicked his tongue once, twice, considering his options. And then he pulled a coin from his pocket. Smiling.

He flicked it, watching the coin spin in the air, under the sunlight. His eyes narrowed as it fell once more, landing on his palm.

Everything depended on lady luck's whim.

Chapter 17

Ella and Brenner walked up the steps of the only opulently furnished office building in Alaska.

Perhaps this was a bit of an exaggeration, but the space reminded her more of her father's mansion than a workspace.

The two of them paused by the bullet-proof, double-thick security doors marked with 209. Ella stared at the numbers, then glanced back over her shoulder, frowning. Her eyes found the building registry, and she scanned the list of small business names.

And there, next to 209, she read *CL Importing*.

"You sure this is it?" she said.

Brenner nodded once. "Tax records show it is a subsidiary of Clyde Enterprises," Brenner said with a snort.

The two of them turned to face the glass doors which looked like they belonged on a jewelry store outside the Bronx.

Brenner glanced through the opaque glass, peering into the space beyond. Neither of them could make out any figures beyond the door.

"See anything?" Ella asked.

He shook his head, and so she stepped forward, reaching out and ringing the doorbell, feeling a faint shiver run down her spine.

They were here to speak with the two brothers who ran an organized crime syndicate back in Nome. Usually, the Clydes stuck to less violent areas of operation. They toed the line and were left alone, for the most part.

But now...

It didn't look good for them.

Ella rang the bell again, listening to the faint sound of chimes from the other side of the glass.

There was a pause, and then she spotted a thin shape appearing on the inside of the glass.

As he drew closer, the figure materialized. His face carried hints of Asian ancestry, with jet black hair and a neat, charcoal-gray suit. He wore round glasses and an easy smile that belonged on the shores of a California beach rather than the Alaskan wilderness.

He adjusted golden cufflinks as he approached the door.

"Recognize him?"

Brenner shook his head.

"Neither do I."

"Guessing he's the hired muscle," Brenner muttered. "Doesn't look like much."

"Looks can be deceiving," Ella advised.

The two of them waited patiently as the man with the dark hair and easy smile reached the door. He adjusted his glasses, reached out with manicured fingers, and pressed a button. There was a buzzing sound, and then his voice echoed out. "Can I help you?"

"My name is Agent Porter," Ella said quickly, flashing her badge. It received no reaction. We'd like to speak with Daniel and Moses."

"Mr. and Mr. Clyde aren't here right now," said the man with a smile. "Can I take a message?"

Brenner scowled. "Their imported Rolls Royce is in the parking lot," he retorted.

The bodyguard's smile became rather fixed. "I don't know what to tell you," he said. "They're not here."

"Open the door," Brenner said. "We can decide that for ourselves."

But the bulletproof-glass door remained closed.

Ella's gaze shifted to the man's right hand. She noticed that he had a small device connected to his ear, and she immediately realized that he was listening to someone else on the other end. After a brief moment, the bodyguard stepped back and gestured with his hand for them to wait.

"You're sure?" he murmured, finger pressed to his ear. "Yes, sir," he said quickly.

He glanced up at Ella and Brenner once more. "Were you two recently in Nome?" he asked suddenly, his eyes narrowing sharply, his posture tense.

Ella felt something strange shift, though, she couldn't say what it was.

She didn't glance at Brenner but could feel him tensing next to her as well.

After a moment, she nodded once. "Yes. We did attempt to speak with the proprietors at their place of business in Nome."

"I see," said the bodyguard. He clicked his tongue.

He was waiting again as if still listening to his earpiece.

Ella looked up, searching for a camera. She spotted a small, hidden glass dome extending from under ceiling stucco.

She paused briefly, looked directly into the camera, and took a risk.

"We're here to speak with you about Lila Hunt."

She didn't look at the bodyguard, who seemed as if he were little more than a puppet for whoever was speaking into his earpiece.

Instead, she spoke at the camera, standing still, staring with her intense, blue gaze at the blinking lens.

There was a pause.

She added nothing further, allowing the two words, the name of the missing girl, to resonate in the cold quiet.

The bodyguard hesitated, turning briefly, a flicker of concern across his face as he spoke into the receiver. He hid his lips with a cupped hand, speaking in hushed tones behind the bulletproof glass.

He looked hesitant. Even fearful. But then he sighed, shrugged, and looked up at Ella again.

He didn't say anything but instead shrugged again. "Guess they wanna talk," he said simply.

He reached out, pressing a hidden buzzer on his side of the interior.

Then the sound of clicks echoed from within the door before the security mechanisms disengaged and the door slowly opened. The bodyguard motioned for them to enter before stepping back to let them pass. Ella and Brenner exchanged wary glances before stepping into the opulent space.

The man carried a sullen, suspicious look as he watched them both. His gaze kept darting to Ella as if he'd decided she was more than met the eye. But when he glanced at Brenner, his fist bunched.

Ella took all of this in without reacting to any of it.

The interior was just as impressive as the exterior. High ceilings, marble floors, and glittering chandeliers lit the spacious room of the apparent office building.

Ella looked around and saw a large painting sequestered at the far end of the room. She squinted. It was a beautiful still life of a bouquet of flowers, but when she looked closer, she realized that the flowers were made up of intricate interlocking machinery pieces, wires and circuits.

The bodyguard swiftly moved back through the space, towards a beaded curtain in the back. The curtain rattled as he pushed it open and held it open with one extended arm, gesturing for them to enter ahead of him.

In his neat suit and glasses, the man almost looked like an accountant rather than a killer. But his steely muscles and the low body-fat percentage evident in his high cheekbones suggested this man was a threat.

But Ella and Brenner pushed through the beaded curtain, emerging in a smaller, equally ornate office space beyond.

The room was dimly lit, with a single desk dominating the center of the space. Behind the desk sat two men. They were both bald, with rough facial hair and sharp eyes that flicked up to focus on Ella and Brenner as they entered. But apart from their lack of hair, the two looked very dissimilar. One was large, rolls of fat drooping over the side of his chair where it looked like he was too much bread shoved into a small, wooden pan. This man wore an open shirt, revealing chest hair. His brother, on the other hand, was tall and sharp-featured. Not handsome but exaggerated. As if his ears, nose, and eyes had continued to grow long after the rest of his face had settled. His oversized features gave him an owlish quality, but his eyes were tinted with a meanness rather than wisdom.

The Clydes.

"Sit," the skinny one said gruffly, gesturing to the chairs opposite their desk.

Ella and Brenner exchanged a glance, before moving to sit down. The bodyguard lingered, standing awkwardly in the entryway for a moment before turning and retreating back through the beaded curtain.

The Clydes watched him go before turning their attention back to Ella and Brenner.

"What's this about?" one of them demanded.

"We're investigating a missing person's case," Ella said, keeping her tone calm and even. "A girl by the name of Lila Hunt. We have reason to believe you may have information that could help us."

The Clydes exchanged a glance, and Ella could see a flicker of rage pass over their features. They were dangerous men, used to getting their way. And it was the name Lila that had unlocked the door out front.

The Clydes exchanged another glance, before leaning back in their chairs and folding their arms.

"You two like causing headaches?" inquired a voice, drawing Ella's attention back to the desks. It was the larger man. He had a deep, booming, bass voice that almost caused the wooden desk between them to tremor.

Ella and Brenner remained seated. Brenner didn't so much *sit* as remained perched on the edge of his chair, as if preparing to leap into action at the slightest provocation.

But neither of the Clydes seemed intent on violence.

At least not *yet*.

Instead, they were both studying Ella closely. Again, she felt as if they were sizing her up.

"You look familiar," said Daniel, the overweight one.

Moses, whom she recognized as the one with large eyes and ears, leaned forward, glaring at her with those unnerving, unblinking eyes. "You look *real* familiar," he snapped.

Ella sighed. "You likely know of my sister, Priscilla. Porter," she added, though it pained her to mention her family name.

Both men blinked then leaned back.

Suddenly, Moses grinned, his lips peeling back like old taffy. "I see... So this is a shakedown, huh? Why not say so. How much does she want? Is it your old man? Betcha it is. Fine... Jameson gets his cut. I never said no-way otherwise. How much this time?"

Ella blinked, taken aback by this sudden inference. She didn't know anything about a *cut* for her family, but she wouldn't put it past her father to use his power in Nome to keep some of the smaller enterprises in line through threats and extortion.

She shook her head, though. "The similarity in our appearance is where it ends. I don't represent my family. I'm here for the Bureau." Neither of the Clydes looked convinced, though. Both were smirking, nodding their heads knowingly.

"I'm afraid you don't quite understand," Ella said firmly, sitting up straight in her chair and folding her hands on the table. "We're not here to offer you any kind of deal. We simply want information that could lead us to Lila Hunt. If you have that information and you're willing to provide it, we can make this quick and painless. If not, we'll have to find another way to get what we need."

The Clydes exchanged another glance before Moses leaned back in his chair, studying Ella with a scrutinizing gaze. "And what makes you think we have any information about this girl?" he asked, his tone icy.

"Because we know that you had some dealings with her in the past," Brenner interjected, his voice low and gruff. "We have reason to believe that she may have been involved in some... activities, and we know that you two have your fingers in a lot of pies in Nome. If anyone has any information that could help us, it's you."

Daniel chuckled then, his lips pulling back in a sneer. "You think we're involved in illegal activities? You think we're criminals?" he asked incredulously.

Ella raised an eyebrow. "I think you know exactly what we're talking about," she said, her voice steady. "And I think you have information that could help us. And like I said, if you're not willing to provide it, we'll have to find another way to get it."

The Clydes fell silent then, studying Ella and Brenner with an unreadable gaze. Ella held their stares, refusing to back down. She had dealt with dangerous men before.

Even the mention of her father's name brought back more than one painful memory.

But Ella studied these two men. Were they who she thought they were?

She pictured the figure on the security footage she'd seen on their boats. The one who'd brushed past the victim.

Ella frowned at them.

"What do you know about Kennicott?"

"What?" said Moses.

"It's a ghost town," replied Daniel, studying her.

Ella's eyes moved to Daniel. "So you do know it?"

"Heard of it. Shopping around for a location to conduct... business." He flashed a smirk, showing a golden tooth.

Ella sighed. "And when's the last time you were there?"

"No clue. Never been. Just had a surveyor. Didn't fit our needs."

"Likely," Brenner said, his tone clearly one of suspicion.

"And what does that mean?" Moses demanded.

"Means we found your burial ground," Brenner shot back.

The moment he said it, the brothers tensed. "This is a murder rap?" Daniel asked slowly. "You found Ms. Hunt's body?"

Ella didn't reply. Was he intentionally playing dumb? If so, it had been a quick response. She couldn't tell if he was being deceptive or not.

She fidgeted uncomfortably, biting her lower lip. But she then leaned forward, staring between the two of them. "We know Lila Hunt was dealing for you. At the school."

"Dealing what?"

"Cards?" Moses guessed.

"Drugs," Ella replied. "And we know she had meetings with you back in Nome. We saw her on your camera."

"And was that before or after you broke into our office and were caught trespassing on camera?" snapped Daniel, leaning forward now and turning his phone for her to see. "We recorded it, Ms. Porter. And you did not have a warrant."

He showed her a video of herself. Ella grimaced as she watched the screen.

She had been careless. They had been caught on camera. She had hoped they could keep their presence in Nome low-key, but clearly, that was not the case.

"We had reason to believe that Lila might have been in danger," Ella explained, trying to salvage the situation. "We were simply checking to see if you had any information that could help us."

Daniel scoffed. "You expect us to believe that?"

"We're not here to convince you of anything," Brenner spoke up, coming to Ella's defense. "We just need answers. And if you're not willing to provide them, we'll have to take matters into our own hands."

The Clydes exchanged another glance, clearly weighing their options. Ella held her breath.

Finally, Moses leaned forward, his expression serious. "Listen, we don't know anything about any murder. We're small time. You know that.

At least, if you did your homework, you do. Lila wasn't our choice. She came to us. For help, I should add."

Ella's heart jumped at this new information. "What do you mean she came to you for help?"

"She wanted out," Daniel explained. "She was tired of living the posh life—as in out of her daddy's big ol' mansion. The government gig, she said, wasn't all it was cracked up to be. She wanted to start fresh. We had connections that could help her. But before we could make any arrangements, she vanished."

Ella studied them carefully, trying to gauge their sincerity. They seemed genuine, but she had learned not to trust anyone too easily.

"Can you tell us more about these connections?" she insisted.

Moses sighed, leaning back. "Do I gotta do all the work for you? Thought you were the cop."

Ella's patience was wearing thin with these two. "Just answer the question, please," she added, sticking to her trademark patience in the face of snark. Brenner just rolled his eyes.

Moses exchanged a look with Daniel before finally giving in. "We have connections to some big players in the game. Word on the street is that Lila was trying to make a deal with them too. Anything to get away from Daddy. Get my gist?"

"And who are these big players?" Brenner asked, his voice dripping with suspicion.

Moses shook his head. "I can't tell you that. But I can tell you that they're dangerous. And if you think you can just waltz in there and get what you want, you're in for a rude awakening."

Ella leaned forward, her eyes boring into Moses's. "We don't plan on waltzing in there. But we need to know who these people are. Do you have an alibi for the time of Lila's disappearance?"

"Yeah. But unless you come with more than chatter, I ain't givin' you shit."

"Besides," Daniel cut in. "What's this gravesite you said you found in the ghost town? Did you find her or not?"

Ella didn't answer. If he was the killer, he would've known Lila was not found in the Kennicott Ghost Town. Her remains hadn't been in the bone pile. But again, she couldn't be sure.

Still, Ella just shrugged. "We're turning over every stone."

Daniel snorted. "Good luck with that. If she is dead, which we still can't confirm, you're dealing with the big leagues. These guys don't mess around."

"We'll take our chances," Brenner said firmly. "Where were you when Lila was kidnapped?"

"What time was it?" Daniel snapped.

"Why don't you just walk us through your movements over the last couple days."

"Hey! Casper!" Daniel called waving towards the beaded curtain. The bodyguard ducked his head back in. "You got the travel logs from Mickey when you were out?"

Casper nodded once.

"Bring 'em. Get these pigs off our tails, will ya?"

Casper nodded quickly and turned.

Ella looked back at the brothers. "You can account for your where-abouts?"

"Yeah. Of course. This isn't our first rodeo, sugar. We know your type. You ain't gonna pin a murder rap on us." He frowned. "We're businessmen. Besides, kinda rich coming from you. Your old man's twice as bad as anything we are."

Both brothers nodded firmly.

Ella couldn't disagree. Instead, though, she simply said, "Let's see your itinerary. And we can take it from there."

Chapter 18

Ella tapped her chin pensively, shivering as she stepped from the plane, back onto the tarmac in the makeshift airfield outside the Kennicott Ghost town.

Brenner followed behind her, also frowning, also lost in thought.

The two of them had been glued to their phones. Going through the itinerary and GPS locations of the two vehicles that transported the Clydes over and over again.

Accounted for. Not only that, but security footage from inside the vehicles confirmed the two low-level criminals hadn't been anywhere near Lila's school when she'd vanished.

Brenner was speaking on the phone now. "I'm very sorry for your loss. You're sure? She'd been to Nome before?"

Ella glanced back, listening in under the cover of night as the two of them stood on the asphalt.

She noticed a dark SUV parked on the other side of the chain-link fence. For a moment, she thought she spotted two figures watching her.

She frowned in their direction. But then the SUV rolled up its windows and began to drive away, moving slowly.

She felt a faint flicker of a frown crease her features.

Two gunmen had come after her back in Nome. Brenner had nearly been burned in his own apartment by those thugs.

She shivered faintly and felt Brenner wrap an arm around her, even as he continued his phone call. "We don't have anything," he said. "I'm sorry." And then he lowered the phone. "She hung up," he muttered.

"Our victim's mother?" Ella asked, glancing at him and picturing the smiling DMV photo of the murder victim they'd found in the basement of the old saloon. Her eyes traversed to this building. It stood out like a silhouette.

The SUV had disappeared now, and her attention was drawn to a small group of FBI agents by the front steps of the old saloon. Figures were arguing, gesticulating wildly.

Someone was saying in a loud voice, "What do you mean he's gone missing? Agents don't just go *missing*. Where the hell would he have gone?"

A long pause, quieter responses, but then another outburst. "The plane that left? Why the hell would he sneak out on a hidden plane?"

Ella frowned at this part, sharing a look with Brenner. The two of them began moving towards this gathering of federal officers. Someone was missing?

And what did they mean about a hidden plane?

She and Brenner strode hurriedly towards the figures.

"Not the mother," Brenner said, answering her question from a while ago as if his brain was on lag. "She couldn't bring herself to talk. Was the sister."

"Oh."

"Yeah. Oh."

The two of them trailed off, both frowning.

"Clydes could easily have hired someone," Brenner said. "Nothing in their financials," Ella replied. She frowned. "Besides... he really didn't know one of the bodies here wasn't Lila's."

"Or he was bluffing."

"He would've had to be a *really* good actor."

"He lies for a living, Ella. It's what they do."

She sighed but shrugged. She couldn't disagree with this. She held up three fingers, lowering them one at a time as she listed, "Their GPS is an alibi. Their bodyguard vouches for their whereabouts, and they didn't seem to know anything about Lila. Not to mention the texts."

"Right..."

Brenner scowled, and Ella glanced down at her own phone, re-reading the texts they'd managed to pull from Moses Clyde's phone.

Texts from Lila. They didn't seem like a threatening set of messages, though. Nearly two months ago, the governor's daughter had reached out. And it had almost seemed... like she'd been applying for a job.

The text simply read, "I need out. This is Lila Hunt. Look me up. Pic attached. I think I could help you. I need some cash. Can I come meet?"

It was a bold, confident message for a teenager to send a crime boss. Or maybe just foolish... Sometimes, people lived their whole lives without hearing *no;* they assumed they were entitled to the world.

But Ella re-read the message, checking the date. The curt replies all seemed cordial, if a bit veiled.

It didn't look like the text exchange between someone and their kidnapper. And if it had been a blackmail play, then it had simply fallen into the Clydes' lap. Lila had reached out to *them.*

But why?

Her father... That's what Moses and Daniel had said. Her father, the governor of the state, was something... extra.

Ella frowned, still moving towards where the small gathering of FBI agents were arguing.

"We need to send out a search party. Find Agent Hamlin."

"He's probably just taking a nap somewhere," another man replied, slapping his gloves together to discard flecks of snow and ice.

Ella's eyes darted to the man as he spoke and she noticed the look of frustration on his face.

"Excuse me," Ella interjected, stepping forward. "What's going on here? Why are you searching for Agent Hamlin?"

The five agents turned to her. She didn't know any of them personally. One of them stepped forward. "We're searching for Agent Hamlin," he said, "He's gone missing and we have no idea where he's pissed off to." The man rubbed his hands together, shivering and glancing around.

Ella's frown deepened. She turned to Brenner, who looked equally troubled by the news.

"Do you have any idea who saw him last?" Brenner asked Agent Collins.

"I did," said a woman with dark hair and dark eyes. She had a tan that seemed out of place in the barren cold. "He's my partner. He went off to take a leak. Never came back."

"Hard to believe," muttered the bearded Collins.

But he went quiet when the woman gave him an angry glance.

"We're canvassing the town," Collins said quickly, "But so far, we've found nothing. It's like he vanished off the face of the earth."

Ella's mind raced as she thought about the missing agent. Was it possible that he had been taken by the same people who had taken Lila Hunt?

She gnawed on the corner of her lip, glancing towards the mountains. "You said something about a hidden plane?" She grimaced apologetically. "Sorry, just, we overheard."

"Yeah," said the female agent. "Parker," she added, giving a small, cursory wave.

Ella nodded back in greeting.

"After you two left," Parker said, nodding at Ella and Brenner, "Another plane took off. A smaller one. It took off from one of the iced-over lakes in the mountains."

"Hang on, what?" Ella said, frowning.

But the woman was nodding adamantly. "Another plane took off. Small thing. We tried to radio it, but no one answered."

"I didn't see any plane," Brenner said.

The woman nodded. "It left only a bit after you did."

Ella and Brenner were both frowning incredulously at each other now.

"What type of plane?" Brenner said.

Ella's mind was spinning with all the disparate questions, and she was starting to get a headache.

"A single-engine Cessna. It was white with green stripes," Parker replied, her eyes scanning the wilderness around them, clearly distracted. "But it wasn't Hamlin," she added quickly.

"Seems like... it could've been, right?" Brenner said slowly. "If he's missing and a strange plane took off..."

"No," Parker insisted. "How would he have had a plane just randomly hidden up here? Besides, he's terrified of flying. Trust me," she added, wrinkling her nose as if at some rough memory.

Ella nodded, her brain working double-time to piece together all the information. A missing agent, a hidden plane, and a teenage girl who reached out to a criminal boss for help. It was a complicated puzzle, and she wasn't sure if they had all the pieces yet.

But one thing was clear, they needed to find Agent Hamlin.

"He wouldn't have just wandered off," Parker said, brushing a hand through coal-black hair, and shaking her head as she kept her voice low and urgent. "We're in the middle of a damn investigation. We need all hands on deck. He wouldn't have."

The boss, Collins, just shrugged noncommittally. The other agents gathered around kept their peace as if they'd already volunteered as much information as they were comfortable sharing and now pre-ferred silence.

"This plane," Ella said suddenly, "It left immediately after us?"

Parked nodded.

Ella felt another shiver, but this had nothing to do with the cold. What the hell was going on here?

If somehow the killer and kidnapper had taken this agent... then the Clyde brothers really couldn't have had anything to do with it.

Ella shook her head, biting the inside of her lip in the hope that the pain might help her focus.

She glanced back towards the ghost town. She looked toward Collins. "Are any of your agents in an SUV patrolling the airfield?"

He blinked, hesitated. Then shrugged. "Not sure, why?"

She shook her head. "No reason." But inwardly, she kept thinking about the hitmen who'd been sent after her... Words like *the Architect* and *the Collective* kept resonating in her head, but this case wasn't connected to any of that. And in a way, she was grateful for it.

She sighed after a long moment, adjusting her sleeves and turning to face the town. "We can have some of us search the buildings. Others can grid search the surrounding mountains. We'll find him," she added to Parker, giving what she hoped was a comforting smile.

It wasn't returned.

Parker and Collins began directing the other agents. Ella and Brenner began to move through the dark, both of them frowning as they approached the saloon.

"Might as well start here," Ella muttered.

"You want a second look at the murder scene?" Brenner whispered under his breath.

"That too."

Chapter 19

The Ghost emerged from the darkness, a phantom blending seamlessly into the shadows that cloaked the abandoned Kennicott Ghost Town. This was his playground, and tonight, he had come with a singular purpose—to blow this forsaken place off the map. The thought sent a shiver of anticipation down his spine.

"Let's get to work," he whispered to himself, his voice barely audible above the howling wind.

He glanced back at the mountain pass where he'd landed... A quick trip. His pilot's license had come in handy more than once and not just as a poacher. Now... he'd been able to follow those agents. See where they'd been going.

And intervene... though they didn't know it yet. No one did.

He smiled, adjusting his gloves.

The Ghost was an enigma, his face obscured by a black balaclava that left only his piercing eyes exposed. He moved with a fluid grace, the kind that spoke of years spent honing deadly skills in the rugged wilderness. His lean figure was clad in the uniform of an FBI agent: a dark navy blue jacket bearing the iconic emblem on one side and a crisp white shirt beneath it, tucked into perfectly pressed trousers. A holstered Glock pistol rested against his hip, completing the image of an authority figure not to be trifled with.

"Time to blend in," he muttered, his breath misting in the frigid air.

His gloved hands expertly checked the straps of the backpack he carried, ensuring that its precious cargo of dynamite remained secure. The weight felt reassuring against his back, like a ticking time bomb waiting to unleash chaos upon the unsuspecting town. He couldn't help but smirk at the irony of it all; here he was, dressed as an agent of order amidst the ruins of a town he intended to tear apart.

"Let's make some noise," the Ghost said, his voice low and determined.

As he began to move deeper into the town, his footsteps were silent, leaving no trace of his presence. He knew the stakes were high and the danger ever-present, but that just made him more resolute in his mission. With each step, he reminded himself of the potential consequences if his plan were to fail: capture or death, neither of which he was willing to accept.

"Focus," he told himself, his eyes scanning the deserted buildings for any signs of life. He paused, pulling out a coin, fingering it in his gloved hand. He frowned at the item, tossed it in the air, and caught it again. Heads.

He smiled and doubled his pace.

Midnight cloaked Kennicott Ghost Town, the inky blackness swallowing the abandoned buildings whole. A chill wind howled through the empty streets, stirring up the long-forgotten dust that had settled on the ground. The decrepit remains of the once-thriving mining town stood as silent witness to the ominous events unfolding before them; dark windows like gaping mouths waiting to swallow any intruder whole.

The Ghost whispered but without words, like the sibilant hiss of some serpent, pulling his FBI standard-issue jacket tighter around him. He glanced at the notable landmarks - the crumbling Kennicott Mill and the skeletal remnants of the old railway system - each casting eerie shadows in the faint moonlight. He couldn't help but shiver, not just from the biting cold, but from the unnerving atmosphere that permeated the air.

His mind raced with thoughts of FBI agents lurking in the darkness, ready to pounce at the slightest hint of suspicious activity. He knew the danger he faced as he prepared to plant the dynamite around the town while blending in with the very people who were trying to stop him.

"Hey, Jackson!" a voice called out, causing the Ghost to stiffen. "You got any updates for us?"

"Negative," the Ghost replied, smoothly adopting the name he'd given to a couple of the sentries. A name that didn't belong, but the different teams from different alphabet-soup agencies didn't communicate as well as they should. Now, many of them were searching the mountains, looking for a body they'd never find. "Still searching for any signs of our guy!" the Ghost replied, gruffly.

"Keep your eyes peeled," the other agent said, his voice tense. "Still no sign of him. They're starting to think the worst. Something about a plane."

The Ghost hid a smirk. Even the plane they'd spotted—*his* plane—had been pinned on their missing agent.

"Understood," he answered, feeling sweat bead on his forehead despite the frigid air.

As he moved stealthily through the town, planting the explosives with swift, practiced hands, the Ghost was acutely aware of the perilous balance he maintained. One wrong move could send everything crashing down around him, both figuratively and literally. He paused at the saloon, pressing one of the sticks under an awning, shoveling dust with his foot to obscure the red material.

His heart raced as he rigged the last stick of dynamite, the imminent explosion echoing in his mind. The Ghost felt a thrill at the thought of his plan coming to fruition, but he knew that now was not the time for celebration.

Time to get out of here, he thought, glancing around for any signs of nearby agents. The game was far from over, and he couldn't afford to let his guard down just yet.

The wind howled through the deserted streets of Kennicott Ghost Town, rattling the shutters of the dilapidated buildings and sending a chill up the Ghost's spine. The air was thick with tension, every creak and groan from the decaying structures threatening to expose his deception. He could taste the metallic tang of fear on his tongue, mixed with the dry dust that billowed around him.

He pressed on, taking in the eerily abandoned storefronts and rusted mining equipment as he navigated the town's twisting paths. His footsteps echoed ominously against the backdrop of silence, broken only by the distant whispers of other agents searching for him.

In this game of cat and mouse, there was no room for error—he had to remain focused. The Ghost paused, adjusting his grip on the pliers hidden in his pocket, and took a moment to steady himself.

As he moved through the maze of crumbling structures, his senses sharpened, his ears straining to catch any hint of approaching danger. The cold seeped through his jacket, numbing his fingers as he fumbled with the fuses on the dynamite. Time seemed to slow, each tick of the clock weighing heavily on his chest as he calculated his next move.

"Jackson! What's your position?" an agent's voice crackled over the radio, causing the Ghost's heart to skip a beat.

"Near the old church," he responded, trying to keep his voice steady. "Haven't seen anything yet."

"Copy that," the agent replied. "Be careful."

"Roger that," the Ghost said, a bead of sweat trickling down his temple.

He fought to maintain his composure as he continued weaving through the town, narrowly evading capture at each turn. The adrenaline coursing through his veins fueled his determination, driving him to push forward even as the danger mounted.

Shadows lengthened. The Ghost paused. A floorboard creaked.

"Damn," he muttered, eyes darting. Howls of distant wolves pierced the night air.

"West side clear," an agent announced through his earpiece. Closer than before.

"Copy that," another replied. Their boots crunched on gravel, just around the corner.

The Ghost held his breath. Heart pounding. Time slipping away. He needed to move—now.

"Did you hear that?" a nearby agent whispered.

"Probably just an animal," the other responded, unconvinced.

"Stay sharp," their leader ordered. "He's here somewhere."

"Roger that," the agents murmured in unison.

The Ghost exhaled, silently cursing his luck. He edged forward, staying low. Avoiding detection was critical. Failure wasn't an option.

"Control, we've got movement near the mine entrance," an agent reported. Goosebumps raced down the Ghost's spine.

"Proceed with caution," Control instructed. "He could be armed."

"Understood," the agent said, determination lacing his words.

He retreated a few steps, and then paused, frowning.

As he stood in the shadows of the alley, waiting for the agents to pass, he spotted a familiar face.

A face that defied the odds.

The blonde woman who looked *identical* to her twin.

Ella Porter. He'd looked them up on his short flight to Juneau and back.

She was striding towards the saloon, next to a tall man with grim features.

The two of them were holding a whispered conversation as they hastened through the dark.

He swallowed briefly, staring after them.

The FBI agents who'd been searching the street moved off again. He waited for them to pass.

The dynamite was set.

The fuses were rigged to respond to a remote detonation. But the dynamite could go off at any moment... he needed to leave. Get on his plane. That was the plan... to watch it all go up in smoke as he flew away.

But his luck had held out this far.

And she was right *there...*

He stared after her, with something close to lust and hunger in his gaze.

What were the odds?

He stood in the shadows. Flipped a coin.

And smiled.

He began to move, stalking from the dark, chasing after where the two agents were slipping into the saloon.

A building he'd already planted an explosive at.

And none of them knew a thing.

The moon cast eerie shadows in the deserted streets of Kennicott Ghost Town as the Ghost slunk through the darkness, his heart pounding like a metronome. He knew he had to act fast, but with every turn and twist in the labyrinthine alleyways, the risk of discovery grew.

No one called after him, though.

No one knew a thing.

He chased after the two agents, racing towards the saloon, excitement in every step.

Chapter 20

Ella stood quietly in the basement of the saloon, staring at the portion of the ground where a body had been found only two days before.

She shivered, rubbing her hands absentmindedly along her arms.

Brenner came stomping down the stairs, sending up small clouds of dust from the wooden steps. He shook his head as he approached. "Nothing upstairs."

Ella was staring at the ground in the corner, her eyes lingering on a dark stain on the wood. "I see," she murmured. "He's not here either."

Brenner said nothing.

The two of them just went quiet for a moment.

An FBI agent was missing. At least eight girls were dead, and the governor's daughter was still missing.

The Clyde brothers had a solid alibi, and Ella felt as if she were canoeing without a paddle.

She glanced back at Brenner. "What do you think they meant about the governor?"

"Hmm?"

She frowned. "The Clydes. They said Lila wanted out. That her father was a piece of work."

Brenner stared at Ella. "Careful now," he said quietly. "Some bells can't be unrung."

"I'm just asking a question."

The two of them now faced each other. Brenner was glancing towards the stairwell as if worried someone might appear and overhear.

But when no one came, he just sighed, shrugged, and shook his head slowly. "I mean... government jobs are always hard. Constant criticism. Gotta bend some rules sometimes."

"I get that, but I mean..." Ella bit her lip. "But why would his daughter go to a couple of drug dealers to get out?"

"I don't know."

"Yeah. Me neither."

"Could ask the Clydes."

"I didn't get the sense they knew either. Felt as if they were just playing coy to string us along."

"So maybe they're just bullshitting us." Brenner shrugged.

Ella began to reply, but a shadow moved past the window behind them. She went quiet.

The shadow disappeared.

For a moment, prickles crept up her spine. The two of them stared quietly at the window.

But no one appeared again. Feds were searching the ghost town, the mountain, everyone looking for the missing agent and any more burial sites.

It was all a mess.

Ella felt as if she were in a cat and mouse game, where she was the mouse.

"So what are you saying? What's the play?"

"I mean... maybe we talk to the governor himself..." She shrugged.

"You think that's the call?"

"Why not?"

Brenner chuckled. "Because he's the governor."

Ella's eyes narrowed.

"It's not..." Brenner began but trailed off, rubbing the back of his head.

"What?" she demanded.

"No... Nothing."

"No, what were you going to say?"

"Nothing," he said more firmly. But then, he sighed. "I'm just saying, it's not your dad. I know you have a thing about authority figures... especially the ones that look corrupt."

"And the ones who mistreat their daughters," Ella added, feeling a flash of temper, but she concealed it just as quickly.

Brenner didn't call her on this emotional suppression this time. Instead, he just shrugged. "I just mean you don't wanna kick over every hornet's nest."

"I know that," she murmured. "Really, I do. But what if he knows something he's not telling us. What if she's not kidnapped? What if she's just in hiding?"

"Odds of that when the victim we found in this basement is her exact lookalike?"

Ella shivered. "Yeah... fair point. Still... I think we should use the SAT phone to call the governor. Talk to him a bit."

"Governor Hunt won't take lightly to that."

"I know."

Brenner eyed her but shrugged. "I'll back your play, Porter. Just hope you know what you're doing."

Ella nodded, determination settling in her bones.

Brenner's expression remained serious. "Alright. I'll get the SAT phone ready. But remember, be careful. We don't know who we're dealing with here."

Ella took a deep breath before nodding, the gravity of their situation settling in. They were in over their heads, but they couldn't give up. Not when there were still innocent lives at stake.

As Brenner set up the phone, Ella couldn't help but think about the governor's daughter, Lila. She wondered if she was still alive, and what kind of horrors she had endured at the hands of whoever had taken her.

But there was no time for idle thoughts. As soon as the SAT phone was ready, Ella took a deep breath before connecting the number through the Bureau's channels.

With shaky hands, Ella dialed the number for the governor's office. She was put on hold for what felt like an eternity, but finally, Governor Hunt's assistant picked up.

"May I ask who's calling?"

"FBI, Agent Ella Porter," Ella said, trying to keep her voice steady.

A tense silence. "Is this in regard to the governor's daughter?"

"Yes. I need to speak with Governor Hunt."

Another pause. "I'll see if the governor is available."

The hold music started again. Ella felt her anxiety building. What would she say to the governor if he did answer? How would he react to her questioning him about his daughter?

But before she could dwell on these thoughts for too long, the other line clicked and a deep voice filled her ear.

"Governor Hunt speaking."

"Hello, Governor Hunt. This is Agent Ella Porter. Thank you for taking our call."

There was the sound of a clearing throat on the other end of the line. "What can I do for you, Agent Porter?"

"We were wondering if we could speak to you about your daughter, Lila," Ella said, holding her breath.

There was another pause, longer this time. "I'm sorry, Agent Porter, but I'm afraid I cannot comment on an unsecured channel. What office are you out of?"

Ella frowned briefly.

Brenner, who could hear as well, gave a strange look.

Neither of them spoke for a moment.

The governor's tone was odd. As if he were simply on a business call. There was no urgency. No fear.

Just a calm, relaxed tone.

Ella began pacing in the basement now, striding rapidly back and forth.

"We're out of the Nome field office, Governor Hunt," Ella replied, her voice steady despite her nerves. "I understand your concern for security, but we're in dire need of information regarding your daughter's disappearance. We have reason to believe that she might be in danger."

"I appreciate your concern, Agent Porter. And have you found any leads yet?" the governor answered in the same calm tone.

"We're following up some leads," Ella said cagily.

"I see."

Another long pause.

Ella shared another look with Brenner.

Hunt began again, his voice low, firm, full of rich tones and a confident cadence, very much a politician's voice.

"I understand that you're trying to do your job, but I can't discuss matters related to my family with unauthorized personnel. I have a meeting... Is that all?"

Ella gritted her teeth, feeling anger rising within her. How could he be so nonchalant about his own daughter's safety? "Sir, I understand your reluctance to speak with us, but we need your cooperation in this matter. Your daughter's life could be on the line."

There was a pause, and Ella could feel her heart pounding in her chest. Finally, the governor spoke again. And this time, there was a note of irritation in his voice. "Agent Porter, my answer remains the same. I can't discuss my family matters with strangers. If you have any pertinent information that could help in finding my daughter, I suggest you bring it to the *proper* channels."

And with that, the line went dead. Ella stood there in silence for a moment, staring at her phone in disbelief.

"That went well," Brenner said.

"I felt like I was a telemarketer," Ella replied. "You'd think I was trying to sell him kitchenware."

"It is suspicious."

The two of them drifted off into silence. Ella was shaking her head, feeling a coldness descend on her. And then she nodded once.

She raised the phone and began dialing.

"Who now?" Brenner said.

She looked at him over the phone, the screen glowing beneath her.

"His wife," she said. "Lila's mother. Let's see if she's as cavalier."

Chapter 21

The Ghost stared through the glass window, peering down at the two figures inside. His hand fidgeted with something in his pocket, gripping his phone and tracing his fingers over the metallic surface.

His eyes had narrowed to slits as he watched the two figures within.

They didn't see him.

Didn't know him.

It was enough to send pleasurable shivers down his spine. His phone could remote detonate the dynamite he'd placed throughout the abandoned town, and now he itched to do just that.

But not until he had a shot at *her*.

The odds were stacked against him. But when had that ever mattered?

He stared at the beautiful, blonde woman inside the basement. She was pacing back and forth, placing another call.

Who was she calling this time? He frowned, scratching at an ear and glancing down at his own phone again. He cleared his throat and then stood to his feet, shivering in the cold.

The old, abandoned saloon was like some towering juggernaut of splintered wood and moldered boards. He moved hastily towards the entrance, propelled by excitement.

As he stepped inside, the air was damp and musty, but it was the unyielding darkness that made him pause. The silence was deafening, with only the creaking of the old floorboards beneath his feet to keep him company. His grip tightened around the phone in his pocket, while the other hand clutched a small flashlight. The beam of light from the flashlight only illuminated a small area, making it difficult to navigate through the maze of empty rooms.

He heard a noise coming from one of the doors and made his way over, keeping a low profile as he approached the entrance which led to the basement. For a moment, he paused, taking in the old, dusty, expansive area. He'd been here before, of course.

When he'd left *her* downstairs. Her luck had run out. He could now make out their voices from the basement. He inched forward, the anticipation making his heart beat faster.

He could hear her breathing now, soft and steady. His hand reached inside his pocket and gripped the cold metal of the knife. He took a deep breath and pushed open the door ever so slightly.

He peered down the steps, staring directly at the two figures at the base of the stairs.

The blonde woman was standing in the corner of the room, phone in hand. He peered through the brief opening in the door, just watching.

He could hear his own breathing now, heavy and labored. More of a pant, really.

Sweat had prickled along his upper lip, but he didn't lift a finger to wipe it away.

Lila Hunt.

He heard her mention the name.

She kept mentioning it.

His eyes narrowed. He'd moved on from Ms. Hunt. Why couldn't they?

Perhaps it was because he hadn't *given* them what they'd wanted.

A body.

A corpse for them to play with and prod and examine.

It made them feel so special to stare at the dead. A latent accusation existed between the living and the perished—I'm alive, you're dead, what'd you do wrong?

Yes... yes, maybe he needed to bring them Lila as a corpse. She wasn't far. No... no, he'd brought her with him.

She'd won the game of darts they'd played. Won blackjack. A lucky little girl.

But luck always ran out eventually.

Suddenly, at the base of the stairs, the tall man shifted, turning to face the door.

The Ghost held his breath, darting back behind the frame.

He froze, waiting, listening.

"Hey, who's up there?" came the man's gruff voice.

For a moment, the Ghost just froze, shivering. He licked at his lips. They'd recognize his voice, so he had to disguise it. He called out, "Agent Johnson! Still searching. You two find anything?"

He waited, wincing tentatively.

There was a long pause then the response, "Not yet! You?"

"No! I'll check the building next door!" the Ghost called.

He took a few steps away from the open door, his heart racing. Would the marshal come up and investigate?

He stood in the shadows, staring at the gaping opening, like some monster's maw. But no one emerged.

The Ghost waited, his grip on the knife tightening. He was running out of time. His phone beeped, a reminder that the dynamite was still waiting for his command. He took a deep breath and tried to calm his nerves, considering his options.

He could blow up the town now, or he could bring Lila Hunt here... Trade her in for the newer model.

He grinned at the door, picturing the pretty blonde lady.

But just then, as his mind whirred, he heard a voice.

"Hello, Mrs. Hunt, my name is Agent Porter. Do you have a moment?"

Hearing her voice. A soft but firm tone... it was like a spell was cast, entrancing him.

He approached the door, listening intently, his heart in his throat.

Chapter 22

Ella paced in the basement, doing her best to keep her frown from affecting her tone.

The voice on the other end of the line was a marked difference from the first conversation.

Unlike her husband, Mrs. Hunt spoke with a quavering, urgent tone. "Is there any news?" she said, stammering. "P-please... Did you find her?" A swallow. A curse. "I heard... I heard there was..." A sob. "Was there...?"

Ella wasn't quite sure where this line of questioning was going, but she cut in before Mrs. Hunt could terrify herself any further through unvoiced speculation.

"Ma'am," Ella said quickly, "We haven't found your daughter. But I have a few questions about your husband if you don't mind."

Brenner blinked in surprise at this. Normally, Ella wasn't one to just come out and be direct in such situations, but Ella was tired of the stalling.

She felt as if time were ticking rapidly by, and her thoughts were on Lila.

Maddie, Ella's cousin, was the same age as Lila. The two of them had even been acquaintances in school. What if someone had taken her cousin? What would Ella have done then?

And so she didn't allow herself to slow, or her voice to quaver. Instead, she said, firmly, "Mrs. Hunt, I know this is a lot to ask, but I need to know about your husband's relationship with your daughter. Did they get along?"

"My... husband?" A pause.

"Yes, ma'am. Have you spoken to him recently?"

"No... No, he's out of town. He's often away for his job."

Ella detected a note of resentment in the woman's voice.

"I see... So, did your husband get along with Lila?"

Mrs. Hunt's response was hesitant, her voice catching as she spoke. "Yes, they got along well... at least, I thought they did... May I ask what this is about? Why these questions?"

"Just following every lead, ma'am. We're concerned for your daughter."

A sob that was bitten off after a brief second. "Is she..." Then a redirect. "My husband is a careful man, Agent. He's got his own people looking for our daughter. Do you think we'll find her?"

Ella sighed. She could hear the fear in the woman's voice. "I believe we can still find her, ma'am," Ella said, cautiously. She didn't want to give false hope to this grieving mother.

The chances for Lila were looking slimmer by the hour.

"What do you mean you *thought* they got along?"

"I... It's nothing. I'm sure it's nothing."

"Anything can help us, Mrs. Hunt."

There was a long pause, and Ella didn't interject, deciding to allow Mrs. Hunt to reach her own conclusions. The gravity of the situation hung heavy on the call. The woman gave a brief sigh. Then, after a sniff and a sob, she said, "It's just... But... but lately, things have been different. My husband has been acting strange, almost like he's obsessed with Lila. I can't understand it, he's never shown any signs of this kind of behavior before."

Ella texted a quick note on her phone as she listened, her eyes narrowing in concern at Mrs. Hunt's words. "Can you tell me more about what you've noticed, Mrs. Hunt? Anything that might help us understand what could have happened to Lila?"

There was a brief pause on the other end of the line, and then Mrs. Hunt spoke in a low, trembling voice. "It's hard to explain... but my husband has been fixated on Lila's appearance lately. He's always talking about how grown up she looks, how beautiful she is. It's like he can't stop looking at her."

Ella frowned deeply at this, her mind racing with possibilities. "I see," she said, jotting down another note. "And when was the last time you saw your husband?"

"It was last night," Mrs. Hunt replied quickly. "He was supposed to be home by midnight, but he never showed up. He drives or takes boats—since he's terrified of flying. So it's not unusual for him to arrive late, but I've been trying to call his cell phone all morning, but there's no answer."

Ella's heart began to pound in her chest at this revelation. She knew it was possible that Mr. Hunt was simply avoiding his wife's calls, but a deeper part of her worried that there was more.

"Mrs. Hunt, have you noticed any changes in your husband's behavior before last night?" Ella asked, her voice gentle yet insistent.

There was a long pause before Mrs. Hunt responded. "Well, now that you mention it... he's been very secretive lately. He used to tell me about his work, but now he won't discuss it at all. And he's been staying out late or disappearing for hours at a time. I thought he was just stressed about work, but now..."

Ella nodded, jotting down more notes. "Thank you, Mrs. Hunt. This is very helpful. We'll do everything we can to find Lila and bring her home safely."

"Is... is he involved?" said the woman, her voice turning to a whimpering sound.

"We are simply following every lead, Mrs. Hunt. Please don't jump to conclusions."

"But did he hurt Lila?" she said, her voice louder now, firmer. There was something like a mama bear's growl in it.

"We are investigating every possibility, ma'am. I need to go. Thank you for your time."

Ella hung up the phone before she could do any more damage. Could Mr. Hunt be involved in Lila's disappearance? Was he the one who had taken her? Or was this all just a coincidence?

Ella frowned.

"So you think the governor is involved?" Brenner asked, looking at her.

Ella paused, frowning. She then glanced up the wooden stairs towards a door ajar at the top. She frowned. They'd closed the door, hadn't they?

Distracted, she said, "No. No, I don't think so."

"Wait, really? After hearing that? Sounds like her old man might've been crushing on his own daughter."

Ella looked at Brenner. "Possibly. And maybe that's why Lila wanted out, but think about it for a moment. He's afraid of flying. That's what she said."

"So?"

"Best way to reach this place is by plane. And it's hours from his headquarters by plane. If he was dumping bodies here, there'd be long stretches of time where he was unaccounted for. For a governor?"

Brenner frowned. "Huh. So you don't think it's him?"

Ella was pacing in the basement again, tapping a finger against her lips.

She let out a flicker of a sigh. "I... I think I need to clear my head. Go for a walk."

"Want company?"

"From you? Sure..." She winked to show she was teasing. But then her tone sobered. "I think I should just take a moment. Is that okay?"

"Sure. Whatever you need. Just, you know, stay safe."

Ella leaned in, giving Brenner a quick hug.

Then, her thoughts scattering and retracting, her heart pounding, she moved towards the creaking, wooden steps of the old saloon which led away from the murder scene.

She took the stairs one at a time, her frown deepening with every step.

She had missed something. Something major, but she couldn't quite put her finger on what.

And it felt as if time was almost out.

Chapter 23

Ella reached the top of the stairs, frowning. She stepped foot into the open space of the old saloon, glancing up at the wooden rafters, draped in cobwebs like mistletoe. The floorboards creaked underfoot as she walked towards the exit.

What was she missing?

The governor was a creep... was that all?

Perhaps his daughter had threatened to blackmail him. Or perhaps his comments had been entirely innocent and misconstrued because of poor phrasing. Perhaps his daughter was spoiled and overreacting. Her friends back at school hadn't spoken very highly of Lila.

Ella sighed, rubbing a hand over her face as she approached the wooden counter, where years ago drinks would've been served to the miners who'd come up for air.

Her finger trailed in the dust on the old, worn surface, leaving a faint streak.

She wrinkled her nose from a few stray particles that tickled the inside of her nostrils.

Scratching at her lip, she stared at the surface of the table.

"What was the plane?" she said, speaking aloud to no one in particular.

A plane had followed them from the mountain pass around the same time the FBI agent had disappeared.

Why?

Had it been the agent?

The killer?

Where was the plane now?

And why had it followed them?

She shifted uncomfortably from one foot to the other, her mind moving in quick, jolting patterns, trying to keep track of all the information presented to her.

Had the person been in Juneau at the same time as them? They'd only spoken to the Clydes and then returned.

So if someone had followed them, they'd kept their distance...

Unless, again, she was missing something.

She pictured the figure in the dark hood on the boat. The one they'd seen on security footage, bumping into Lila Hunt.

"But the governor is afraid of flying," Ella murmured under her breath, her brow furrowing.

She shifted from foot to foot, shaking her head and peering over the bar at the old, dusty shelves.

She took a second to scan the old, abandoned saloon. She felt isolated, cold. Her eyes moved along the wooden counter and ventured over to the remnants of glass shelves.

She paused, breathing slowly, thinking through her options. What was she missing?

Some piece... some crucial component of all of this was missing.

She wracked her brain, forcing herself to focus.

She held out a single finger against the rough wood of the countertop. "Not the Clydes, but associated. Knows how to fly a plane, potentially." A second finger came out as she marked off the evidence. "Encountered at least two of the victims on the brothel barge back in Nome." A third finger. She frowned. "Poaching background. Or smuggling." She gnawed on the corner of her lip.

She replayed conversations in her mind, one at a time.

The governor seemed an unlikely place to settle. Terrified of flying.

Lila's mother had seemed very concerned. Of course, she ought to have been. But why was this bothering Ella?

Concern?

And then it settled on her. As she stood there at the counter, staring at the glass across from her, she spotted her own reflection.

The way she fidgeted, shifting side to side, she thought of the Clydes' office in Juneau. The opulent furnishings contrasted by that big, bullet-proof glass door.

Someone had followed them to Juneau by plane, but Ella had never seen them...

Unless she had.

"Concerned... very concerned," she murmured to herself. "He was very concerned when I mentioned Lila Hunt."

She could picture his face now. The widening of the eyes, the sudden hesitation. She'd thought it was because his boss was chewing him out...

But what if it was because he thought they were on to him?

She felt a prickle across her skin. Her face flushed, and her heart pounded.

And as she stared at the glass, and as her mind zeroed in, focusing, she went still.

"You got those travel logs from Mickey when you were out?"

Not *when you were out,* meaning, while you were outside. But out... when he was absent.

The question had been addressed to Casper, the bodyguard. The doorman in those glasses with that suit, who'd tried to prevent them from speaking to the Clydes. In fact, he'd been adamant that they leave... And he hadn't seemed surprised to see them there. Now, Ella could remember how his gaze had lingered on her, watching her... very closely.

She felt another shiver.

The bodyguard had been on leave. Had been absent. Until when?

That morning?

When he'd come back by plane, following them?

He'd been concerned over the mention of Lila's name. He'd seemed to recognize Ella and Brenner, and he had been on a leave of absence, it had sounded like.

Plus... someone in the organization with the Clydes would've had access to Lila. Would've had access to the brothel barge to encounter the girls, like the figure on the security footage.

Ella found her breath catching, and she turned around, staring towards the door to the basement.

Was she completely mistaken?

No... No, she didn't think so.

It made sense.

She'd have to verify. What had his name been? Casper?

She pulled her phone with a shaky hand from her pocket. Did he have a background in poaching? Hunting? Military training?

She quickly used her phone to access the federal DMV database. Known associates of the Clydes... She typed *Casper* then hit *enter*.

Immediately, a face she recognized appeared. He was wearing the same glasses he had been back in Juneau.

Casper Nguyen.

He had a series of small-time arrests back in his teen years. Arson. Dealing.

But nothing since.

At least, nothing he'd been caught on. She frowned, staring.

Except one thing.

She clicked a link, following it. Illegally selling grizzly pelts.

She stared at the information.

Pelt-selling... Like a hunter might? A poacher?

She shivered. Someone who might know the terrain out here. Who would be able to fly a small Cessna and land in known terrain without trouble? Someone who was used to avoiding detection...

She stared at those dark eyes behind the glasses and felt her body tense.

"It's you," she said, staring at the image. "Shit. It's *you*. She spun around, approaching the basement again in a small jog. "Brenner!" she called out. "Brenner!"

No reply.

She frowned, pausing at the top of the stairs, peering into the basement.

He hadn't come up after her.

But the lights were now off...

"Brenner?" she called, a bit louder.

Still no reply.

What the hell?

She felt goosebumps along her arms. She took a hesitant step onto the stairway.

The wooden steps creaked beneath her boots as she descended into the dimly lit basement. She sensed a presence, a feeling of foreboding, but she pushed it aside. She had to find Brenner.

As she reached the bottom of the stairs, she heard a muffled sound, then a faint groan. She paused, holding her breath, listening.

There it was again, a soft thump, like something heavy hitting the ground.

"Brenner?" she called out, louder this time, moving cautiously towards the source of the noise.

The deeper portions of the basement were large, with shelves of crates and boxes lining the walls. She could hear her boots striking the concrete floor with each step.

She spotted a faint light, coming from around the corner. She moved closer, her heart pounding, her body tense.

As she approached the light, she realized it was coming from the soft glow of a flashlight which now rested on the cold floor; she saw a figure lying on the ground next to the light.

Brenner.

He was face down, bleeding from the back of his head. Someone had struck him. His hands were tied behind his back. She could see the ropes digging into his wrists, and she felt a surge of anger.

"Brenner!" she called out again, rushing towards him.

As she reached him, she could see that he was unconscious. She knelt beside him, her hands trembling, trying to untie the knots.

That's when she heard a sound behind her, footsteps approaching. She turned, her heart racing, and saw a dark figure emerging from the shadows.

He pointed the gun directly at her.

"Don't move," he whispered, his breathing heavy.

She turned slowly, her fingers slicked with Brenner's blood. She turned to face him, hands extended, eyes widened.

He leered at her, his face like a Jack-O-Lantern. He was wearing a dark ski mask that hid most of his features.

"Well, well," he whispered. "Looks like I trapped a mouse."

"Casper Nguyen," she said quietly. It wasn't a question.

And for a brief moment, the man behind the ski mask blinked as if taken aback. Then his eyes narrowed.

He reached up, pulling the mask off, staring at her.

She recognized his features. Sharp cheekbones, no glasses now—hair slicked back. He wasn't wearing the neat, charcoal gray suit any longer, but had rather opted for an FBI agent's uniform. Likely the uniform of the missing agent.

She stood in front of Brenner's fallen form, facing the poacher in the basement of the old saloon.

"So you knew it was me?" he said, voice tense. He dropped the ski mask to the ground and quirked an eyebrow. "What gave it away?"

Ella Porter's breath came in ragged gasps as she stared down the barrel of Casper's gun, her heart pounding in her chest. The cold, Alaskan wind whined outside, a stark reminder of the icy death that awaited her if she couldn't find a way out of this mess.

"It doesn't have to end like this," she whispered, her voice barely audible above the howling wind.

Casper smirked at her. "Bad luck, I guess. You should've thought about that before you stumbled onto my territory, sweetheart. Alright, listen up, Ella." Casper spat her name like it was poison on his tongue. "You're gonna do exactly what I say, or I'll have no qualms about leaving your pretty, little corpse out on those mountains for the bears."

Ella had always been resourceful, but her current situation left her feeling trapped. She glanced at Brenner once more. For someone to have snuck up on the Ex-SEAL, they would've had training themselves.

She stared at Nguyen.

"Fine," she managed to say, somehow keeping her voice calm, her gaze never leaving the gun aimed at her heart. "What do you want me to do?"

"Smart girl." A cruel smile twisted Casper's lips. "You know... you're one of the lucky ones."

"Oh?" she said hesitantly. She decided if he was talking, it meant he wasn't shooting.

He just nodded. "Yeah... I've seen your sister. You two look so alike. Made it easier for me than usual. Do you know how hard it is to find them?"

"Find who?"

"The matches. The odds-defiers." He frowned at her. "You don't get it, do you? Natural selection. Chance. It's all the same. Luck... it all boils down to luck."

Ella didn't reply. She had to survive—and to do that, she needed to stay focused and look for an opportunity to escape or turn the tables on her captor.

"I can't say I feel too lucky in this moment," she said slowly.

He smirked. "Funny. Now come with me, or I shoot your boyfriend."

She kept herself between Brenner and the psycho with the gun.

"Lead the way," she said, her voice steady despite the terror clawing at her insides.

"We're going outside first," he said. "Don't try anything. I mean it. I've got an itchy trigger finger."

She kept her hands raised and allowed him to prod her up the stairs, back from where they'd come.

"Want to see something fun?" he asked, smirking.

"What's that?" she said, her voice nearly lost in the howl of the wind coming through the ghost town.

"I left a little present for you feds. Check it."

Casper paused as he stepped from the door and indicated something lodged under the extended base of the wooden railing.

She blinked, staring.

And then her eyes widened.

Two sticks of dynamite and what looked like a remote detonator strapped to the bundle.

Ella felt a wave of panic wash over her. It wasn't just about her survival anymore—she had to stop Casper. There were people nearby... not to mention...

She swallowed, scarcely daring to think it through. Brenner was in the basement.

"What are you planning to do with that?" she asked, keeping her tone steady, focusing on the remote detonator.

Casper chuckled darkly. "Watch the fireworks, I suppose. And you'll watch it with me, my dear."

It was a sick game to him—one that Ella couldn't allow him to win. She quickly scanned the area, looking for options. There was a wooden toolbox a few feet away, maybe she could use it as a shield or a weapon.

But before she could make her move, he snatched at her arm, yanking her forward.

She stumbled a bit, wincing at his vice-like grip.

"Move!" he whispered fiercely. "No—not that way. You think I'm stupid. They're searching over there. This way. Now! We're going to play a game."

With a self-assured stride, Casper led Ella through the ghost town, away from the saloon, approaching the treacherous mountain terrain. As they walked, he seemed to know every rock and crevice intimately, as if the mountains themselves had whispered their secrets in his ear. The ghost town's presence cast an ominous shadow over the landscape.

"You know, I've been coming up here for years," Casper said, his voice echoing across the desolate expanse. "Started out as a hunter but soon realized there was a lot more money in poaching." He looked back at her, winking.

Ella gritted her teeth, her heart thumping in her chest. It felt as if they'd been walking for far, far too long. The minutes stretched. Time seemed to stand still and speed up all at once. Her ears were peeled for the sound of an explosion...

But it never came.

She knew she had to keep him talking, to give herself time to think and plan her escape. "So, what's this game you want to play?" she asked, her voice wavering slightly.

"Ah, yes, the game." His eyes glinted with a twisted excitement. "You see, I've always been a fan of chance. There's something so... exhilarating about leaving your fate to the whims of Lady Luck."

He paused, turning back to face Ella. "And that's what we'll be doing today, Ms. Porter. A little game of Three-card Monte to determine whether you live or die."

As they approached a decrepit building in the mountains, Ella frowned. They'd moved past a bluff, which had almost seemed to hide this small alcove—almost like a hidden valley. She certainly hadn't seen this space before, nor had she seen what occupied it. Not just the strange, squat wooden structure. But also an old plane, hidden in the shadows of the mountain. Its once-shiny metal exterior now dulled by years of exposure to the harsh, Alaskan elements. "We'll play right he re."

He approached the flank of the plane, gesturing at her with his gun.

She came slowly, her eyes darting about, looking for something... anything she could use as protection.

"Come here!" he snapped, tapping his gun against the plane's wing.

Ella reluctantly approached, trying to keep calm and focused. As she got closer, she noticed that there were three cards laid out on the top of the plane's wing. She tried not to stare but also tried not to glance back... So far, no sound of explosions from behind her.

But anything might set Casper off... and with him, his explosives.

She glanced back at the cards, wondering how far she could go with humoring him before she had to *do* something rash.

The cards were turned over, so she couldn't see what was on them.

"Casper, I don't want to play this game," she said, her voice firm.

He just chuckled. "I think you'll change your mind when you see what's at stake."

He gestured at the cards. "Pick one."

She hesitated, her eyes flickering between Casper and the cards. She knew that this was a trap, that there was no winning, only losing. But she also knew that she had to keep him talking if she wanted to gain any ground.

"Okay," she said, her voice level. "I'll play your game. But what's the prize?"

Casper grinned at her. "Ah, that's the fun part. If you win, I let you live."

"And if I lose?"

He just shrugged. "Well then, I guess Lady Luck wasn't on your side."

Ella took a deep breath, trying to steady herself. He was watching her closely, refusing to give her an inch of space to make a move.

"I'll pick the middle card," she said, trying to keep her voice calm.

Casper rolled his eyes. "Not yet, idiot. I haven't shown them to you, yet."

Ella was barely paying attention.

But Casper seemed to enjoy this part. And now as she watched him closely, she could see the madness in his eyes.

He was muttering to himself, grinning as he flipped the cards, nodding up and down. "It's all connected," he whispered. "Just like it says. They're all connected." Even as he fidgeted with the cards on the edge of the wing, shaking his head as he did, Ella could hear him saying, "Not right, you know. Two of you. Two of you that share a soul. The same two." He looked up at her, frowning.

"What do you mean?" Ella asked softly. "Is that why you killed the others? Is that why you killed Lila?"

"Who? What... Oh, Lila? No... she didn't die. She's in there," he said, waving a hand towards the plane. "She's good at these games, you know," he said, smirking at her. "Want me to bring her out? You can play against her! Yes... that'd be fun!"

But Ella quickly shook her head. "No... no, that's fine. We can play."

He looked at her, frowning. "Do you think I'm stupid?"

"No," she said simply. *Absolutely, you evil twist,* she thought.

But she didn't pay full attention to his furious gaze. Instead, her eyes moved to the plane. She thought she spotted a figure, hunched over, visible through a greasy window.

A figure who was trembling.

Then a face pressed suddenly against the glass, a pale face with wide eyes. Mist fogged the window as Ella recognized the dirt and tear-streaked features of Lila Hunt, the governor's daughter.

Ella's heart sank at the sight of Lila, realizing that she had become a pawn in Casper's sick game. She knew she needed to act quickly and decisively if she wanted to save both of their lives.

"Casper, I don't want to play this game," Ella said, her voice steady and firm. "I want to talk to Lila. Bring her out here."

Casper chuckled, his eyes glinting with a manic energy. "You really think I'm that stupid, don't you?"

Ella didn't answer, keeping her focus on the plane. She could see Lila's breath misting up the small window as she tried to communicate something to Ella.

"I'm serious," Ella said, her voice taking on a harder edge. "If you don't bring her out here, I won't play."

"If you don't play, I'll kill you."

"I don't believe you," she said simply, though, it was hard to say it with the gun pointed at her head. "You need this, don't you? You drag the women here... play these games. Why? Have you ever told anyone *why*?"

She could see the rage in his eyes. The hatred. She was pushing him—she knew it. But as she stood there, in the cold, her thin jacket catching gusts of wind and fluttering, she couldn't look away.

The small figure in the plane's window was still shivering, breathing heavily and fogging the glass.

Brenner was still back in a ghost town rigged with dynamite. Perhaps in more than one location.

And she still had a gun pointed at her skull.

Casper's eyes narrowed, but Ella could see him wavering. She pressed her advantage, taking a step back towards the bluff.

"Come on, Casper," she said, her voice coaxing. "You don't want to kill us both, do you? You sometimes let them live... like with Lila.

For a moment, it seemed like Casper was going to let her speak with the governor's daughter. He even glanced towards the window.

But then his eyes narrowed, and he sneered. "We play this game *my* way. Now look! Look, damn you!"

She did, reluctantly. But his hand had been straying for his phone, and she didn't want to risk a detonation.

He peeled the cards back, one at a time, raising them for her to see.

The Queen of Hearts, the Ace of Spades, and the Joker. He set them facedown on the wing of the plane, leaning his foot on a makeshift stool fashioned from a rusty oil drum, and began to shuffle them around, his movements smooth and practiced.

"Here's how it works, Ms. Porter," he said, his eyes locked on hers. "I'll shuffle these cards, and you just have to guess which one is the Queen of Hearts. Pick the right card, and you live. Pick the wrong one..." He let the threat hang in the air, a grim smile playing at the corners of his mouth.

Ella watched the cards as they danced beneath Casper's hands, her mind racing. She had never been good at games of chance, but she knew she couldn't afford to lose this one. Her life—quite literally—depended on it.

If I can just focus, she thought, *maybe I can outsmart him somehow.* But with the gun still trained on her, Ella realized that even if she somehow managed to win this twisted game, there would be no guarantee that Casper would keep his word. And so, as the cards continued to blur together, she searched desperately for any opportunity to turn the tides in her favor.

"Queen of Hearts," Ella said, her voice steady despite the pounding of her heart. To her amazement, she lifted the card—and there it was, the red queen smirking at her from beneath Casper's calloused fingers.

"Beginner's luck," he scoffed, resetting the cards. "Let's see if you can do it again."

As the cards swirled into motion once more, Ella noticed a slight bend in the corner of the Queen. She wondered if it was intentional or if Casper hadn't noticed it himself. Either way, she decided to use this small advantage to her benefit.

"Again, the Queen of Hearts," she said, pointing to the card with the bent corner. Once more, she had guessed correctly.

Casper's eyes narrowed, and his jaw clenched as he realized that he'd been outplayed. The tension thickened around them, the air heavy with suspense and danger.

"Fine," he growled. "One last round."

This time, Ella noticed that Casper had straightened the corner of the Queen of Hearts, eliminating her advantage. But just as the game began, she picked up on another detail: a faint smudge of dirt. With her eyes locked onto that smudge, she followed the Queen's movement and made her final guess.

"Queen of Hearts," she declared, a note of triumph in her voice as Casper flipped over the winning card once more. The frustration on his face was palpable, but so too was his determination to maintain control over the situation.

"Alright, Ms. Porter, you've proven yourself resourceful," he admitted begrudgingly. "But I'm tired of playing games." He reached into his pocket and pulled out an old, tarnished silver coin—a 1921 Morgan dollar. "Heads, you live; tails, you die. Simple as that."

"Wait!" Ella interjected, desperate to buy herself a few more seconds. "I won your game! I won!"

"No... you cheated."

"I didn't. How? I didn't touch the cards."

"Heads or tails!" he snapped. "Now!"

She didn't have a choice, and they both knew it. The gun was still pointed at her, and now, he seemed angry.

Chapter 24

Still standing by the old, rusted plane hidden in the valley near the ghost town, Ella stared at the gun and the silver coin. Desperately, she said, "How do I know you won't cheat?"

"Fine," Casper replied with a sinister grin. "You call it in the air."

As soon as the words left his mouth, he flicked the coin high into the sky, the silver glinting in the moonlight as it spun and tumbled through the air. All of Ella's focus was on that coin, her heart pounding in her chest as she calculated the risks.

"HEADS!" she shouted, her voice echoing through the mountainside.

The silver coin reached its apex, and as it began to descend, Ella made her move. She didn't care about the damn coin, but he seemed to, like an entranced child. And while the coin was at its apex, causing him to tilt his chin, his head back, she made her move.

Her eyes locked on Casper's, she lunged toward him with all the strength she could muster, slamming her shoulder into his chest. The force of her tackle sent both of them crashing to the ground, the gun slipping from Casper's grasp.

"Get off me, you bitch!" Casper snarled, trying to push her away. But Ella was relentless, driven by a fierce determination to survive. She aimed a well-placed knee at his groin, causing him to gasp in pain.

She seized the opportunity to wrench his arm behind his back. Casper's face contorted in agony, but Ella knew she couldn't afford to let up. One wrong move could give him the upper hand.

Casper growled, gritting his teeth against the pain. Ella could see the murderous glint in his eye.

The two of them grappled like wild animals, their bodies slick with sweat and dirt, desperation fueling their every move.

As they struggled, Ella became acutely aware of her precarious position—the edge of a sheer cliff loomed dangerously close, and one misstep would send them plummeting into the abyss. Desperate to gain the upper hand, she shifted her weight and attempted to throw Casper off balance.

But her tactic backfired. In that split second, Casper managed to twist free from her grip, shoving Ella hard toward the precipice. Panic surged through her veins as she felt herself losing control, her feet skidding on loose rocks, teetering on the brink.

"Goodbye, Ella," Casper sneered, lunging forward in an attempt to seal her fate. But as his arms reached out to shove her again, she instinctively grabbed onto him, pulling him down with her as they both tumbled over the edge.

Ella had flung herself to the side, avoiding the sheer drop and instead hitting a slope.

She yelled as she did, pain shooting through her body upon collision.

Casper was near her, and the two of them tumbled in a blur, their shouts piercing the Alaskan air.

The fall seemed to last for an eternity. Ella felt a sickening crunch as her body collided with jutting rocks and craggy outcroppings, pain radiating through her limbs. Through it all, she held onto Casper with a vice-like grip, refusing to let go.

Wind whipped past them, tearing at their clothes and stinging their faces as they plummeted toward the unforgiving earth below, picking up speed as they rolled down the sharp slope. Despite the agony wracking her body, Ella's thoughts were consumed by one burning desire: survival. With every ounce of strength left in her battered form, she struggled to shift her position, attempting to use Casper's body as a buffer against the worst of the impact.

As they neared the base of the slope, Ella's world became a blur of pain and adrenaline, each passing second bringing her closer to the ultimate test of her will to live.

With a deafening *thud*, Ella and Casper hit a row of knobby trees. A cloud of dust swirled around them, their bodies entwined and bruised. As the dust settled, Ella's ragged breaths were the only sound that pierced the silence of the desolate Alaskan wilderness.

"Get... off... me," Casper wheezed, his voice as faint and tremoring as a death rattle, barely recognizable through the pain. He tried to push her away, but the effort was futile; their limbs were tangled together like the Gordian knot.

Gritting her teeth, Ella rolled off him, gasping as she tried to regain control of her breathing.

Ella ignored Casper, focusing on her own body's response to the situation. Her legs felt like jelly, her arms laden with lead. But still, in the recesses of her mind, a stubborn spark of determination flickered, refusing to be extinguished.

She took a shaky step forward, then another, each movement sending jolts of pain through her battered body.

As she stumbled away from Casper's prone form, Ella couldn't help but wonder if he was still alive.

"Wait!" Casper yelled, desperation creeping into his voice. "You can't leave me here!"

Ella hesitated, torn between the desire to save herself and the nagging sense of responsibility she felt toward the man who had tried to kill her. She knew that if their roles were reversed, Casper wouldn't give her a second thought.

"I said stop!" he screeched, whining as he did.

He'd lost his gun in the fall, but he had something else in his hand. An item that was still glowing with electricity.

His phone.

A bent finger hovered over a button. "I'll blow the whole thing up!" he said, glaring at her, blood trickling down his face. He propped his head up against a rock, his back pressed to the stone. "I swear I will!"

She stared at him. He glared back, both of them bleeding, bruised. Her ankle clicked as she tried to adjust her weight. Broken? No... but probably sprained.

"I'll blow it all!" he yelled. "I swear I will!"

She turned back fully to face him now, releasing a long, low sigh.

"Do exactly as I say," he snarled. "Or else." He tried to push to his feet, but his legs were shaky, and one gave out under him. Definitely broken.

In fact, she could see bone jutting through his leg, having punctured his pants. Blood poured down his leg.

He let out a moan of pain, but his eyes were fixated on her, his hateful gaze resolute.

"What do you want me to do?" she said.

He blinked a few times, heaving desperate gasps of air. But then his lips curled into a snarl and he said, "Help me back to the plane. Or everyone dies."

"The plane?"

"You heard me!" he yelled, his voice rasping. "You cheated. It would serve you right for me to blast the place anyway."

Ella wasn't sure what to say... again, he had her trapped.

She glanced back up the slope towards where the plane awaited. Her eyes narrowed.

"Do it now!" he screamed.

She saw no choice.

What would he do when they reached the plane?

But that question would have to wait.

She turned, trudging back towards him, limping on her sprained ankle, breathing heavily. She helped him slowly to his feet. He kept his phone far from her, extending it out with his arm.

He smelled like sweat and rancid blood. Likely his own blood... or perhaps the blood of the man whose uniform he'd stolen.

"Now go!" he demanded, his arm wrapped over her shoulders, sending shivers down her spine.

She allowed him to guide her, moving once more up the slanted ground.

As they moved, she scowled deeply, wanting nothing more than to lash out at him, but his thumb hovered over the button on his phone.

Brenner still wasn't safe.

So she hiked, trudging up the slope she'd just tumbled down, moving towards a plane with a kidnapped girl trapped inside.

And fearing, or perhaps *knowing*, that once they reached the plane, it wouldn't end well for her.

Chapter 25

Behind them, the ghost town glistened beneath the Alaskan moon, a beautiful illusion that belied the terror gripping Ella's heart. Her boots crunched on the snow as she trudged up the mountain path, each breath forming a frosty cloud in the frigid air. Her blonde hair was now pulled back to keep it out of her face. Her eyes darted from side to side, searching for any possible means of escape.

"Keep moving," Casper growled, his voice rough and menacing. He prodded her toward the stationary Cessna, limping as he did and leaning against her. She could feel blood from his side seeping against her abdomen, through her open jacket. His figure cast a shadow over her, sending shivers down her spine despite the layers of clothing she wore.

A sickly smile played on his lips as he watched her struggle to think of a way to take his phone from him. But he kept it extended with his good arm, away from him, his thumb hovering over the middle button as if it were some sort of dead man's switch. "You don't want me to blow up that quaint, little town now, do you?"

Ella gritted her teeth, fighting the urge to lash out at him. She knew that any attempt would be futile while he held the lives of so many innocent people in the balance. His threat echoed in her mind, the image of the remote detonator seared into her memory. Was Brenner still unconscious? The thought of moving in together was now a distant echo.

She'd be content with just *seeing* him again.

"Get in the plane," the pilot ordered, his tone brooking no argument. His eyes were cold, unyielding—so chilling they could have been carved from the glaciers surrounding them. His face was unkempt, and his clothes hung loosely on his frame, portions scraped and dusty or soaked in blood. Despite his appearance, there was an air of danger about him that unnerved Ella more than his phone.

She tried to speak, her mind racing, thinking of *something* to calm him.

The man merely sneered at her desperation and shoved her toward the aircraft.

"Save your breath," he said with a cruel laugh, the sound echoing off the snow-capped peaks around them. "You'll need it up there." He gestured toward the sky with his phone before using it to prod her forward once more.

Ella's heart pounded in her chest as she climbed into the Cessna, her mind racing with thoughts of what lay ahead.

"Sit down and buckle up," the pilot barked, watching her every move with predatory intent. As Ella reluctantly complied, she knew that she had to find a way out of this nightmare and fast. But for now, all she could do was follow his orders and pray for an opportunity to present itself.

Once seated inside the Cessna, Ella caught a glimpse of a figure chained to the back seat. It was Lila Hunt, the governor's daughter. Her long hair was matted and tangled; her eyes puffy and red from crying. Despite her disheveled appearance, there was no mistaking the fear etched into her delicate features.

"Help me, please," Lila whispered hoarsely, her voice trembling as she fought to hold back more tears. She tugged at the chain that bound her to the seat, desperation evident in every strained movement.

Ella's heart wrenched at the sight of the terrified girl, but her own situation left her powerless to offer any immediate assistance.

"Enough!" the pilot snarled, bringing his attention back to them. He climbed into the cockpit, his jaw clenched and his hands gripping the controls with white knuckles. His eyes darted between the two women as he started the plane's engine, the propeller roaring to life. "You'll both do exactly what I say if you want to live through this." His voice was cold and calculated, devoid of any emotion beyond a simmering rage.

"Wh-what do you want from us?" Ella stammered, her voice barely audible over the sound of the plane's engine.

"Silence!" he snapped, glaring at her.

Ella's mind raced with potential escape plans, but the pilot's menacing presence and the threat of the detonator kept her in check. She exchanged a glance with Lila, who seemed to be on the verge of breaking down entirely. The weight of their shared predicament threatened to suffocate Ella, but she couldn't afford to let fear paralyze her now. Especially not with the younger woman watching.

"Listen to me, Lila," Ella said softly, making sure her voice was low enough that the pilot couldn't hear. "We're going to get out of this, okay? Just stay calm and wait for an opportunity."

Lila's eyes locked onto Ella's, and for a moment, it seemed as though a flicker of hope ignited behind her terror-stricken gaze. But before either of them could say anything more, the plane began ascending into the sky, the Alaskan landscape shrinking beneath them as they were carried away by their captor.

"Stay in your seats, or I blow everything up!" the pilot bellowed, his crazed eyes never straying far from his hostages.

Ella clenched her fists, every fiber of her being yearning to fight back, but she knew that any rash actions would only put them both in greater danger. As the plane soared higher and higher, she forced herself to focus on the task at hand: finding a way to save Lila, the ghost town, and herself from the madman who had ensnared them all.

"Put these on," the pilot barked at Ella, tossing her a pair of cold, steel handcuffs. The cuffs glinted in the dim light of the small plane's cabin as they landed with a heavy clunk in her outstretched hands.

As she reluctantly closed them around her wrists, the chill of the metal seeped into her skin, sending shivers up her arms. The cuffs were tight enough to be uncomfortable but did little to restrict her movement, giving her a modicum of hope. She glanced to Lila, who was staring wide-eyed at the cuffs that bound her own wrists.

"Good, now stay put," the pilot commanded, his voice rough and menacing. Ella couldn't help but notice the cruel satisfaction in his eyes.

Outside, the Alaskan landscape was nothing short of breathtaking. As the plane ascended, the snow-capped mountains appeared closer than ever, their jagged peaks cutting through the sky like unforgiving blades. The vast expanse of untouched wilderness spread out beneath them, a stark contrast to the confined space of the Cessna. The view would have been awe-inspiring if not for the circumstances.

Ella's heart pounded in her chest as the might of the plane's engine roared through her ears, drowning out all other sounds. She could feel the vibrations from the engine rattling her bones, making the fear even more palpable. Despite the noise, the pilot's harsh breathing still managed to pierce through it all, a constant reminder of the threat he posed.

In her mind, Ella began to weigh her options, her thoughts racing in time with the beating of her heart. She knew she had to do something before it was too late. But what? How could she overpower the pilot without endangering Lila or the people in the ghost town below?

"Focus, Ella," she whispered to herself, trying to steady her thoughts.

For now, she would have to bide her time and wait for the perfect moment to act. This was a battle of wits as much as it was one of brute force, and Ella was determined not to let Casper win. The stakes were too high, and the life of the man she cared about most hung in the balance.

She began to inch forward slightly, hoping to bridge the gap between the back seats and the front.

But she froze as his eyes darted back.

"Stay put, or I'll blow the whole damn town to smithereens!" the killer's voice boomed through the cabin, his icy glare fixed on Ella and Lila. The veins in his neck bulged with rage, his knuckles white as he gripped the detonator tightly.

Ella felt a shiver run down her spine, her heart pounding even harder now. She glanced over at Lila, whose eyes were wide with terror. The poor girl trembled like a leaf in a storm, her breaths shallow and rapid. Ella knew she had to find a way to get them out of this nightmare.

"Please," Lila whimpered, her voice cracking. "We won't do anything, just let us go."

"Shut up!" the pilot snarled, his attention momentarily diverted by Lila's plea.

As Ella shifted uneasily in her seat, her gaze fell upon an object tucked against one wall of the plane. It was a parachute, its dark green canvas folded neatly and secured with harnesses. Beside it, a small box labeled 'Emergency' caught her eye. Keeping her movements subtle, she slid the box from under the front seat with her foot, careful not to move the rest of her body. The see-through plastic lid allowed her a glimpse of the contents. Inside, nestled atop a bed of foam, lay a flare gun—its orange and black body gleaming beneath the dim cabin light.

For a moment, Ella's mind raced with thoughts of potential escape plans. The parachute could provide a means of jumping to safety, while the flare gun might serve as a distraction or a weapon. But she also knew that any attempt to fight back or flee would come with considerable risks.

"Remember, one wrong move and it's all over!" the killer barked, bringing Ella back to reality.

His words only served to heighten the tension.

In the midst of her turmoil, Ella caught a glimpse of her own reflection in the window. Her eyes were drawn to her hands, cuffed together in front of her body. She frowned, realizing that the cuffs were not as tight as they appeared to be. She'd intentionally left gaps while she'd cuffed herself. In fact, there was enough slack for her to slip one hand out if she angled it just right.

"Hey," Lila whispered, her voice barely audible over the hum of the plane's engine. "What are you thinking?"

Ella glanced at Lila, who looked both terrified and hopeful. She hesitated for a moment, weighing her options. If she revealed her discovery, would it make Lila feel safer or more alarmed? In the end, she decided that any chance of escape needed to be explored, even if it seemed slim.

"Look," Ella said softly, nodding toward her loosely cuffed hands. "I think... I might be able to get out of these."

Lila's eyes widened, but before she could respond, the killer shouted from the cockpit, "Quiet back there!"

Heart pounding, Ella turned her attention inward, silently working through her options. If she managed to free her hands, what would her next move be? The parachute remained a possibility, but there were two of them and only one parachute. And what about the flare gun? Could she wield it effectively against their captor?

Think fast, Ella, she urged herself, as fear and determination waged a fierce battle in her mind.

With each passing second, Ella became increasingly aware of the risks involved with her potential actions. If she mishandled the flare gun, it could escalate the situation or even set the plane ablaze. Conversely, trying to share the emergency parachute could result in a deadly freefall. A seasoned adrenaline junkie herself, Ella had no idea what experience, if any, the governor's daughter had with skydiving.

And yet, doing nothing would guarantee their doom.

"Okay," Ella whispered to Lila, her voice barely audible. "I'm going to try something. Just stay calm and be ready."

Lila nodded, her eyes filled with a mixture of fear and fierce determination. As Ella prepared to make her move, she knew that there was no turning back. Their lives now hung in the balance, and every choice carried the weight of life or death.

Ella's heart raced as the sound of wind howling outside the plane filled her ears, the thin air above the Alaskan mountains seeming to almost choke her. Her breaths came in short gasps, and she could feel the cold sweat forming on her forehead.

She crouched, poised, just about ready to act...

But then he turned, glancing back at her, his bruised and battered features fixated on hers.

She went still, tense, like a butterfly pierced to a bit of corkboard.

He was watching her now and smiling.

Chapter 26

Ella's heart raced as she stared at the killer, the muscles in her jaw tightening. The plane hummed beneath their feet, punctuating the tension between them. He leaned in close to her, a sly grin playing on his lips, revealing crooked teeth.

"See, Ella," he said, "life is all about luck. I've defied the odds and here we are, soaring through the sky." His breath was hot and stale against her face, making it difficult to concentrate on anything other than the urge to recoil. But she pushed the revulsion aside, focusing on the task at hand—saving Lila.

"Luck has something to do with it," Ella murmured, her voice barely audible over the drone of the engine. She glanced at Lila, her bound hands and fear-filled eyes. "But it's your choices that brought us here."

The killer threw his head back and laughed, a wild, unhinged sound that echoed through the cabin. "That's what my father used to say," he sneered. "Before he won the lottery. Changed his tune then, didn't he? Liked big dreams then... Of course, those dreams involved a pretty-young-thang! He left us all behind. Bad luck, right?"

Ella studied him, her gaze unflinching despite the fear clawing at her insides. "What happened to you?" she asked, her voice softer now. She needed to stall. One of her hands was roaming towards Lila's cuffs, kept out of sight so he couldn't see it.

"Life happened, sweetheart." Casper ran a hand through his greasy hair. "Dad took the money and ran, leaving me with a monster of a stepfather who made every waking moment hell. Foster homes weren't any better. No one cared about me, and now no one will care about your precious Lila either."

Ella clenched her fists, anger surging through her veins. She knew she couldn't let him get under her skin, but the thought of anyone hurting a defenseless teenager made her blood boil.

The killer's eyes narrowed, the grin slipping from his face as he glared at her with unbridled hatred. "You think you can save her?" he hissed. "Just like my father thought he could save himself? No, Ella. I've learned that the only way to truly defy the odds is to take control of them. And today, I hold all the cards."

As the words left his lips, a chilling realization settled over Ella—this man had nothing left to lose. A desperate, unhinged killer was far more dangerous than she'd anticipated. But she couldn't afford to give up now.

A bead of sweat slipped down Ella's forehead as the killer's attention was momentarily fixed on the plane's controls. She had spent countless hours learning to slip out of handcuffs during her training, a skill she never thought she'd need in real life. But now, with the cold metal biting into her wrists, she had no choice but to rely on those long-forgotten lessons.

With a subtle flex of her wrists, Ella managed to loosen the cuffs just enough to slide her hand free from where she'd left it loose. Her heart pounded in her chest as she glanced at Lila, who looked back at her with wide, terrified eyes. With a slight nod, Ella signaled Lila to remain quiet and still.

"Did you think I wouldn't notice?" The killer's voice sliced through the tense silence as he turned his head slightly, watching them from the corner of his eye. Ella's heart skipped a beat, but she saw the opportunity—he wasn't looking directly at her hands.

"I noticed her in Nome. You two both had doppelgangers. Both of you defied the odds... Think you're luckier than everyone else, right? Well... how lucky do you feel now?" He smirked, looking back out the window.

Ella mouthed a silent "Trust me" to Lila before swiftly reaching over to work on Lila's handcuffs.

Lila seemed to understand Ella's plan, and her gaze shifted quickly between Ella's hands and the killer. As Ella struggled to manipulate the lock, Lila subtly moved her wrists to give Ella better access.

The cuffs clicked open, and Lila's breath hitched, but she covered it up with a cough. Casper spared them a glance but, apparently satisfied that nothing was amiss, returned his focus to the controls.

Ella's mind raced as she considered their next move. They were free, but they still needed to disarm the killer and regain control of the plane. If only she could get her hands on the phone that controlled the explosives...

"Are you two whispering secrets back there?" The killer's voice dripped with menace, and Ella knew they were running out of time.

"Nothing worth sharing," Ella replied coolly, her hands clenched and ready for action. She glanced at Lila, whose eyes were filled with terror.

The plane's engines roared, drowning out the killer's laughter as he continued to taunt Ella and Lila. "You think you're so lucky—so much *better* than everyone, huh?" he sneered, his eyes wild and bloodshot. His hands gripped the controls tightly, knuckles white against the dark leather. The aircraft jolted suddenly, causing Ella's heart to lurch in her chest.

Lila sat rigidly beside her, her face pale and her eyes wide with fear. She tried to hold back a sob, biting her lower lip until it turned a painful shade of red. It was clear the situation was taking its toll on her.

Ella clenched her fists, her nails digging into her palms as she fought to keep her emotions in check. Her gaze locked onto the phone clutched tightly in the killer's hand—the device that held the detonator. If she could just get the phone away from him, maybe they'd have a chance.

Ella's heart raced as she calculated the distance between her and the killer. *I only have one shot at this,* she thought. She glanced at Lila, determination filling her eyes. They had come too far to give up now.

"Hey, you—!" Ella shouted, lunging forward in one swift motion.

With a wild cry, she threw her body forward with all her might. Her fingers clasped around the phone like a vice, tugging it away from the killer's iron grip. He tried to keep his hold on it as she screamed and dug her nails in deeper and deeper. With one final yank, she ripped the phone free from his grasp.

He let out an enraged scream, thrashing about and reaching for the stolen device.

"NO!" he bellowed, his face contorted with fury. The plane swayed as he momentarily lost focus on the controls. Alarms blared, drowning out the roar of the engines, as the aircraft dipped dangerously.

With the phone secure in her grip, Ella knew there was no turning back. She had to protect Lila and the people below from this madman's wrath. Her heart pounded in her chest like a drum as she stared into the killer's eyes, daring him to make his move.

"Give it back!" he growled, desperation lacing his voice.

"Never," Ella spat, her grip on the phone unyielding.

"Fine!" the killer roared and launched himself at her. His fists flew like a hurricane, but Ella moved with lightning speed. She blocked his blows with her free arm while keeping the phone clenched tightly in her other hand.

The cramped cabin seemed to close in around them as they grappled and fought, their panting breaths echoing off the walls. The plane groaned under the strain, its engines roaring a warning that went unnoticed by the combatants.

"Give it back!" he snarled, lunging at Ella once more.

She threw her weight into a punch that connected with his jaw. He stumbled back, momentarily stunned, but quickly regained his footing, though he clearly favored one leg. He gasped in pain as he tried to maneuver—adrenaline providing sufficient numbing for his instincts and fast twitch muscles to take over.

In the chaos of the fight, the plane's controls were struck. A cacophony of alarms blared, and the aircraft dropped, sending a rush of vertigo through Ella's stomach as she and the killer tumbled across the floor. The sudden shift in altitude forced Ella's stomach up into her throat, while her heart pounded so hard she feared it might burst out of her chest.

"Look what you've done!" the killer screamed, pulling himself to his feet. As he reached for the controls, Ella's gaze darted past him, through the windshield, and her blood ran cold. They were heading straight for a mountain.

In a split second, Ella's instincts kicked in, and she reversed her grip on the killer's arm, pulling him off balance. She shoved him forward, away from them into the cockpit. He was shouting, trying to adjust the controls.

But Ella ignored it. She lunged towards Lila, the howling wind threatening to tear them apart as they tumbled against the door, which she'd now pried ajar.

"Grab my hand!" she screamed through the deafening roar of the wind, her voice barely audible. Lila's eyes met hers, wide with terror, her mouth forming silent words, but the force of the gale drowned out everything but the hurricane inside the plane.

Ella reached out, stretching her fingers toward Lila's trembling hand, every muscle straining against the onslaught of the wind. Their fingertips brushed for an instant before Lila's grip tightened around Ella's wrist, their gazes locked together in mutual desperation. With all her strength, Ella yanked Lila close, tightening her arm around the girl's waist.

"Wrap your legs around me!" Ella shouted into Lila's ear, hoping she could hear her over the raging tempest. Lila nodded, her eyes streaming tears that were instantly whipped away by the wind. As she obeyed, Ella glanced back at the killer, who was slumped against the cockpit controls, his face twisted in rage.

She snatched the flare gun from beneath the seat. The parachute from the wall.

She'd jumped before—in fact, it was one of her hobbies. But never while plummeting towards a mountain with someone holding desperately onto her back.

Still... no time to hesitate.

Ella yelled one final time, summoning every ounce of courage she had left. Together, they leaped from the plane, their bodies buffeted by the ferocious winds as they plummeted toward the earth below.

Chapter 27

The world rushed past them in a blur, the ground growing closer with each passing second. Ella held onto Lila tight, praying that somehow, they would survive this fall and the parachute would open. She hadn't had time to check it. But there was no time for regrets now; they were in freefall, with nothing but air beneath them and death closing in fast.

Above them, she spotted the plane screeching overhead, the killer still onboard. She stared as the blur of color arched towards the looming mountain.

As she tumbled, wind whipping around her, she gripped at the rip cord on the parachute, adjusting her other hand, which held the flare gun, and pressing tightly against Lila's own hands, making sure the girl was still safely wrapped around Ella's plummeting form.

"Clear from the chute!" Ella tried to mouth. There was no point speaking. Neither of them could hear in the gale.

But now the ground was rapidly approaching.

Ella's heart pounded in her chest as she yanked the rip cord with all her might. There was a sudden jerk, and the parachute billowed out behind them, snapping them back up into the sky. For a moment, they hung suspended in mid-air, the wind buffeting them from all sides.

But they were alive.

Ella let out a ragged breath, her grip on Lila tight as they dangled beneath the parachute. She looked down at the ground far below, her stomach lurching at the distance. But they were safe for now.

She turned her gaze back up to the sky, searching for any sign of the plane.

She watched as it veered up, desperately attempting to avoid a collision.

But the killer had left it too late.

She watched, eyes wide as the plane crashed into the side of the mountain.

A fireball erupted into the air, sending pieces of debris flying in all directions. The sky was filled with the roar of flames and the thunder of falling wreckage.

The explosion sent shockwaves rippling outward, shaking the parachute wildly as Ella and Lila watched in horror. Fire roared up from the wreckage, painting the sky a hellish orange.

Ella felt a lump form in her throat as she realized the full extent of the danger they had escaped.

She held Lila close, feeling the girl's body shake with sobs.

They were alone, stranded in the middle of nowhere, with nothing but the clothes on their backs and a parachute to sustain them.

And one other item.

As they drifted through the sky, Ella pulled the flare gun free.

She aimed it, careful to avoid hitting the parachute.

And then she squeezed the trigger.

Chapter 28

Ella sat trembling in the back of the plane, wrapped in blankets. Brenner reclined next to her, a bandage pressed to his head, his nose wrinkled, but none the worse for wear.

"Why are we flying commercial again?" Brenner murmured at her side.

Ella didn't reply right away. She pictured the plane slamming into the mountain. The giant fireball.

She shivered again and pulled her blanket tighter around her shoulders. She supposed Brenner had a right to be irritated by the airport security checks, the crowded walkways...

But at least they'd sprung for first class.

Now, sitting in the back, hidden behind privacy curtains, Brenner and Ella kept each other warm.

She occasionally glanced out the window at the passing terrain far below, but her mind kept moving...

"Is she going to be okay?" Ella murmured.

"Hmm?"

Brenner shifted, his arm warm against her shoulder.

"Lila... is she going to be okay?"

"Yeah... yeah, she'll be fine," Brenner said. "You really didn't hear all that?"

Ella shook her head. "The chopper that found us was too loud."

"Oh... okay."

He looked disappointed. She glanced at him.

"What?" he said.

"What's wrong?" she returned.

She shifted, pulling the blanket around her, shivering again, and glancing up to make sure the air nozzle was closed above her.

"Nothing."

"You look sad."

"I'm not..." he frowned at her. "So you didn't hear what I said when we found you?"

"I didn't hear anything."

"Oh."

She glanced at him, picturing the helicopter dropping from the sky, having followed the trail of the flare gun. The wreckage of the plane against the mountain had also helped the search and rescue teams locate Ella and Lila where they'd been shivering in a copse of trees, using the parachute as something of a windbreak.

Brenner had been the first off the chopper. And besides the bandage on his head where he'd been struck by Casper, he'd seemed fine.

Now, though, he looked troubled.

He leaned back in the airplane seat, biting his lip briefly, and looking as if he wanted to say something.

"What?" she said again. "What did you say?"

"I just thought... I thought you'd heard me is all."

She glanced at him, quirking an eyebrow. He was acting oddly.

Brenner looked away, then looked back at Ella. "It's nothing, really. I just said... I said that I was glad you were okay and that I was sorry. Sorry for what happened to you, for putting you in danger."

Ella's heart ached. She had never seen Brenner like this before. He was always so confident, so sure of himself. But now, he looked vulnerable and scared.

"T-thank you," she stuttered, not knowing what else to say. "I'm glad you're okay, too. And you didn't put me in danger."

They fell into an uncomfortable silence, each lost in their own thoughts. Ella kept thinking about the crash, about how lucky they were to be alive. She also thought about Brenner, and how much he had risked to save her and Lila.

"I need to tell you something," Brenner said, breaking the silence.

Ella turned to face him, her eyes wide. "What is it?"

"I love you, Ella," Brenner said, his voice barely above a whisper. "I've loved you for a long time. And I know I don't deserve you, but I can't help how I feel."

He looked as if he'd just bared himself and was standing naked before her.

She glanced at him. Shrugged. "I know."

He blinked.

She grinned to show she was teasing. "Of course I love you, too. I thought that was obvious."

Brenner looked as if he had just won the lottery, though perhaps this comparison was one Ella would retire.

Still, she smiled at him, then leaned in slowly, her lips brushing his.

Brenner returned the kiss, deepening it, his hand tangling in her hair. Ella's heart raced as she responded, falling into the feeling of Brenner's lips on hers.

In that moment, nothing else mattered. Not the crash, not the danger they had faced, not even the fact that they were flying commercial.

As they pulled away, their foreheads touching, Ella knew that she loved Brenner more than when they'd been teenagers—things were deeper now, more mature.

"I can't wait to get home," Brenner said, his breath warm against her cheek.

"Me too," Ella replied, smiling up at him. "Are we... are we still moving in together?"

"Yeah. I mean... if you're okay with that."

"I am something of a traditional girl," Ella said, wiggling her eyebrows.

He snorted. "Weren't so traditional in bed... twice. No, wait, three times."

"Three times for *you*," she muttered. "Doesn't count."

He snorted and kissed her again.

She felt the warmth of his lips, the softness of his skin, and his tough, calloused fingers against the slope of her chin.

Shivers spread through her, and for a moment, fear and doubt lifted like the clouds they were now flying through.

Epilogue

Ella stood in her motel room, glancing towards the bed where Brenner lay under bunched sheets.

She smiled at where he slept, his tousled hair caught by the heating unit spewing warm air through the small space.

A motel... she'd been in a motel for some time now. It was time to move.

Brenner hadn't seemed to mind... but if they were going to do this, she was determined they do it properly.

She slowly placed the cup of water back onto the counter by the sink, wiping moisture from her lips with the back of her hand.

And that's when the knock came at the door.

She frowned.

Another tapping, insistent knock.

She stared, approaching slowly.

Brenner stirred in his sleep but didn't wake up. Ella peered through the peephole, her heart racing with a mix of fear and curiosity.

A man with gray features and gray hair stood on the other side of the door. He would've been handsome if his eyes weren't so fully devoid of anything resembling human emotion.

He wore a neat, black suit and black gloves.

Mortimer Graves was standing outside her motel room.

And it wasn't just Mortimer.

He had something in his hand, holding it up for her to see.

His phone.

And on it... a video feed.

"We need to speak, Eleanor," Graves said quietly.

She stood frozen to the spot, peering through the keyhole. And there, on the screen, displayed in the movie he was playing for her, she spotted something that made her stomach churn.

Two men... both stripped naked, hog-tied, and chained at the ankles.

Both men were bleeding...

And both looked *identical*. Twins.

"What is this?" she snapped, her voice sounding frail through the door.

He sighed. "The men who tried to kill you. Assassins."

She went quiet.

"And," he said, in that casual, British accent of his, "They both know who the Architect is... So are you coming?"

He lowered the phone, shrugged, and turned, moving away from her.

Ella stood frozen in the door, caught in indecision. She glanced back at Brenner on the bed. Then back through the keyhole. Graves was hastily approaching a parked car.

He'd found the assassins. The men who'd tried to kill her and Brenner...

And they could lead her to the Architect... The pseudonym of a man who ran a secret society of serial murderers. He funded these psychotic killers, helping them to fulfill their twisted game.

Her father was somehow involved... Or at least knew of the Collective.

Now, Ella felt her stomach twist. She stared through the keyhole, frustration mounting.

Graves was slipping into the front seat.

Time was almost up.

Would he kill those men before she could speak to them?

She opened her mouth, glancing back at the bed.

Then cursed, grabbed her jacket, and flung open the door.

What's Next for Ella Porter

When the governor's murder is brazenly broadcast on live television, a secretive society emerges from the shadows, preying on the wealthy and the elite.

As the ominous countdown begins for the next target—her very own father, Jameson Porter—Ella's relentless pursuit leads her to a mysterious figure known only as the Architect, a reclusive billionaire whose dark influence looms large. In a heart-pounding game of cat and mouse, Ella must navigate the treacherous terrain of the Fairbanks Permafrost tunnel, the site of the governor's murder.

She must piece together the clues, outsmart a ruthless enemy, and expose the truth before the final pieces of this deadly puzzle fall into place. Will she unmask the Architect's sinister agenda, or will she become the next victim in a conspiracy that threatens to tear the state apart?

Other Books by Georgia Wagner

The skeletons in her closet are twitching...

Genius chess master and FBI consultant Artemis Blythe swore she'd never return to the misty Cascade Mountains.

Her father—a notorious serial killer, responsible for the deaths of seven women—is now imprisoned, in no small part due to a clue she provided nearly fifteen years ago.

And now her father wants his vengeance.

A new serial killer is hunting the wealthy and the elite in the town of Pinelake. Artemis' father claims he knows the identity of the killer, but he'll only tell daughter dearest. Against her will, she finds herself forced back to her old stomping grounds.

Once known as a child chess prodigy, now the locals only think of her as 'The Ghostkiller's' daughter.In the face of a shamed family name and a brother involved with the Seattle mob, Artemis endeavors to use her tactical genius to solve the baffling case.

Hunting a murderer who strikes without a trace, if she fails, the next skeleton in her closet will be her own.

Other Books by Georgia Wagner

A cold knife, a brutal laugh. Then the odds-defying escape.

Once a hypnotist with her own TV show, now, Sophie Quinn works as a full-time consultant for the FBI. Everything changed six years ago. She can still remember that horrible night. Slated to be the River Killer's tenth victim, she managed to slip her bindings and barely escape where so many others failed. Her sister wasn't so lucky.

And now the killer is back.

Two PHDs later, she's now a rising star at the FBI. Her photographic memory helps solve crimes, but also helps her to never forget. She saw the River Killer's tattoo. She knows what he sounds like. And now, ten years later, he's active again.

Sophie Quinn heads back home to the swamps of Louisiana, along the Mississippi River, intent on evening the score and finding the man who killed her sister. It's been six years since she's been home, though. Broken relationships and shattered dreams exist among the bayous, the rivers, the waterways and swamps of Louisiana; can Sophie find her way home again? Or will she be the River Killer's next victim to float downstream?

Want to know more?

Greenfield press is the brainchild of bestselling author Steve Higgs. He specializes in writing fast paced adventurous mystery and urban fantasy with a humorous lilt. Having made his money publishing his own work, Steve went looking for a few 'special' authors whose work he believed in.

Georgia Wagner was the first of those, but to find out more and to be the first to hear about new releases and what is coming next, you can join the Facebook group by copying the following link into your browser - www.facebook.com/GreenfieldPress

About the Author

Georgia Wagner worked as a ghost writer for many, many years before finally taking the plunge into self-publishing. Location and character are two big factors for Georgia, and getting those right allows the story to flow seamlessly onto the page. And flow it does, because Georgia is so prolific a new term is required to describe the rate at which nerve-tingling stories find their way into print.

When not found attached to a laptop, Georgia likes spending time in local arboretums, among the trees and ponds. An avid cultivator of orchids, begonias, and all things floral, Georgia also has a strong penchant for art, paintings, and sculptures.

Printed in Great Britain
by Amazon